Bones in the Backyard

Holly Holcraft Mysteries, Volume 1

M R Dollschnieder

Published by M R Dollschnieder, 2024.

Published: May 2024

M.R. Dollschnieder

PO Box 340

Llano, CA 93544

ISBN 978-1-964463-00-1

Table of Contents

This book is dedicated to my husband, Kenny, for supporting me in this endeavor and to my dear friend and colleague, Rhonda Arnold, who has been the inspiration for Holly and her adventures.

PROLOGUE

Rain was pelting my face in the pitch black and my shoes sank into the ground with every step I took. My jacket was soaked through by the freezing rain and my hand holding the phone shook so badly I was afraid of losing it. Between the power outage and the rain, my vision was severely limited, the light from my phone reflecting off the rain instead of illuminating the ground but I figured I had to be close to the right spot. It was confirmed with my next step, when my foot sank down in the mud up to my knee. I fell on my hands and knees into the mud, dropping my phone, which landed upright illuminating a tiny skull.

This is a terrible way to get to know me. To begin, let me go back a little bit. It all started with a girls night out at the bar to celebrate my best friend's escrow closing. Escrows can be a bit tetchy at the best of times so when one finally closes, we go all out.

A CELEBRATION

We were at Dagwood's Bar on a Saturday night for a little wine and relaxation. The bar was a little dive in the center of town but it had a comfortable feel to it and it was a nice place to celebrate and forget our worries.

The place was always packed because when you live in a small mountain community, it's one of the few places to gather. We were seated at a small table by the wall and had to put our heads together and shout to be heard over the loud music.

"Holly, who's that pretty girl with Joe?" my friend Lucy White grabbed my arm and pointed to the bar. Rubbing my arm, I glanced at where she was looking.

Giving the girl the once over, I replied, "I don't know. She is pretty though." a petite girl with short brown hair with golden highlights and deep brown eyes. she had the kind of looks that would only get more beautiful over time. "Maybe Joe will get lucky." I crossed my fingers as I said it. Joe has been my assistant for the past six months and I hadn't yet seen him with anyone. Not that his relationships were any of my business, but I like people to be happy.

"Eh, she's okay," interjected Shelby White, no relation to Lucy. Short like me, but with long luscious brown hair that made me jealous. She and I had gone to high school together. Shelby believed that high school was the foundation for everyone's future relationships. It sort of makes sense if you think about it. I mean what years are your favorite songs from? Everyone always refers to their high school sweetheart, they remember their teachers, and reunions always focus around your high school achievements. There are also a lot of regrets from high school plus it makes up most of the crime plots on television.

Our three heads swiveled to look at her. Shelby was nothing if not blunt, and perhaps a tad jealous from time to time and I've just learned to accept her as she is.

Vana raised her eyebrows at her. "Jealous much?"

I've known Vana Dago also for ten years now, ever since I had moved to Appleby. She was very much the sister I never had and didn't know I needed. She was also a fellow real estate agent and the reason we were in the bar celebrating after closing a deal that had lingered on for six months. The septic had collapsed just after escrow had opened and the seller disputed that they should pay, then they continued to use said septic until the whole thing overflowed. It had been a big mess. Ugh.

Shelby waved her hand in the air and took a sip of wine. "Of course not, I just think we have different ideas of pretty."

Vana smiled at me. "How are your taxes coming?"

"You sure know how to ruin a good evening," I replied, taking a long drink of wine.

"Isn't that why we're here drinking? You talk about your troubles and then we drink to it and feel better, freer, like when you write your troubles on a note and then burn it."

"Fine," I sighed. "I've asked for an extension, I'm going to get it caught up, I just need these escrows to close."

Lucy leaned over and put her hand on mine. "They will close, you just keep doing you." Lucy is a title rep I've been working with for a good ten years. We just hit it off one day. She is a gorgeous brunette who should be a model. It's a strange thing but title reps always seemed to be really good looking. Most importantly, she is one of my nearest and dearest friends.

"Vana, you understand what it's like being a real estate agent. You've been one longer than me. The ups and downs and never knowing if a deal is going to close until it actually is recorded." I rested my chin in my hands on the table. "Sometimes, I can't imagine doing this forever."

Vana raised her glass, "Cheers to fortitude and sometimes just plain stubbornness because that's what keeps the real estate world going."

"Cheers," we all said and clinked our glasses together.

"I know it's tough being a single mom, but you did a great job with Penelope and you have a beautiful granddaughter. Chloe is an angel." Shelby smiled at me. Her smile could melt snow and the hearts of most men. "Now if your daughter could just find regular daycare and stop calling you to babysit."

And there she was, the real Shelby White.

I held up my glass, "Cheers to friends who tell it like it is." We all clinked our glasses together once again.

Lucy fiddled in her bag and then handed us each a business card. "Hey, what's this?" I asked.

"Read it silly," she answered.

Lucy White

Title Representative

Morecroft-Appleby Title

"Are you opening an office here?" I exclaimed.

"Yes!" she was fairly bursting with excitement. "It's going to be right on main street next to Katie May's."

"Congratulations!" we all screamed.

"That'll be convenient," commented Vana. Katie May's was a restaurant favorite for our group and we usually ate lunch and sometimes, breakfast and dinner there as well. Not necessarily all on the same day.

"Are you going to move here? I know a good agent," I said half jokingly.

"No, I'll still live in Morecroft but split my time between the two locations. Appleby doesn't have quite enough business to support a full time location but it will let me spend more time with you."

"Good, because I have escrows to close this month, specifically the Marples..."

Vana snorted, cutting me off, "Only if Bonnie stops stalling." Bonnie Belmar was the most troublesome agent I'd ever dealt with. Everything was an issue for her.

I put a smile on my face and took a deep breath. "I will make it work." I said confidently. "Oh who am I kidding. Every file with her is torture. But," I held up a finger. "I am stronger and more stubborn than she will ever be. Cheers to stubbornness," I added, holding my glass aloft again.

"Excuse me." A short, thin man with curly black hair interrupted our cheer. "Are you Holly Holcraft? With the listing on Blackwood Street?" He asked, looking directly at me.

"Yes, that's me."

"My name's Jacob Martin. I'd like to buy that house," he said firmly..

"Well I'm sorry Mr. Martin, but that house is already sold."

He shuffled from one foot to the other nervously. "I thought it was still in escrow. There's no sold sign."

"It is but it's closing soon. It's already been in escrow for over two weeks."

"Yeah, but it's not sold yet right?"

"Well, it hasn't closed yet..."

"Good then," he said, cutting me off. "I want to buy it. I'll offer over asking."

"Mr. Martin..." I began.

"Call me Jacob."

"Okay, Jacob. I stated firmly. "I can't just cancel an escrow because someone else wants to offer more money. We have a contract. If the buyers cancel, you could put in an offer but right now the house is not available."

"But I wasn't in town when it went on the market," he whined. "I wanted it first and Carol bought it out from under me."

Ugh, what is it with people? I mentally screamed in frustration. "I'm sorry but it's not available," I said even more firmly. Jacob got an angry look on his face.

"That's not fair. I'm calling my attorney."

"You do that honey," interjected Shelby. Sometimes she's worth her weight in gold. "If you don't mind, we are having a private party." Jacob gave her a dirty look and stomped off mumbling about his attorney. Shelby looked at me in shock with her brows raised. "Does that happen often?"

"Oh, you'd be surprised. Everyone thinks that what they want is what should happen." I replied frustrated. I raised my glass again. "Cheers to annoying people."

Vana clinked her glass with mine. "Good for you looking on the bright side." Shelby and Lucy joined in with us.

"Shelby, you really should be nicer. He could be a potential client in the future," chastised Lucy. Vana and I looked at each other. "Not mine," we both said together then laughed.

Vana swirled the wine in her glass. "When you start out in real estate, they tell you to take whoever you can get but they're wrong. Life is too short to deal with people like that on a transaction."

"Here, here," I agreed, raising my glass and then taking a sip. Several hours later our little party called it a night and we all headed home.

HOME

What is that awful noise? Did I leave the TV on? My mouth was fuzzy and my brain was not functioning. Running my tongue over my teeth just illustrated how dry my mouth was and that noise! Prying one eye open I still couldn't see but recognized the noise for what it was, my phone alarm, I flung my hand out randomly in the general direction of the noise, my fingertips encountered the edge of the phone and flipped it into the air. Relief and aggravation fought each other for priority as the phone landed with a thud and slid under the bed.

"Aaagghh," emanated from my throat in frustration. I should have said no to the last two glasses of wine previous to the actual last glass. Thankfully, the noise finally subsided and I collapsed back into my pillow.

Lying in my warm, soft bed I slipped back into that wonderful comfortable unconsciousness that comes when you've only got five minutes before the next alarm, which seemed much more like thirty seconds before the noise was blaring again. This time the noise was matched by the dashing of a dog's rather large tongue against my face as my bed shook like an earthquake.

"Blech," I spluttered as the tongue came in contact with the interior of my mouth. "That is just disgusting Ginger. I've told you before no morning kisses!"

Pushing the dog off me, which was difficult because she was huge, I began clumsily extricating myself from the bed covers which were a mess because I don't sleep neat. At 58 and overweight, I was constantly kicking the covers off during a heat flash and then moments later cuddling under them for warmth. Let me just say that menopause is not kind when you don't exercise and like to drink wine and have a passion for donuts. Unfortunately, this extrication resulted in me catching my foot on the sheet and tumbling off the bed, the side of my face unceremoniously smacking the floor. Well at least I found the phone, lying in a nest of dust bunnies, under the bed. Have I mentioned the rather large dog with an unceasing loss of dog hair?

A sudden whump drove the air from my lungs as Ginger ecstatically landed on my back and proceeded to thoroughly douse my face with dog spit.

"No. Ginger we are NOT playing. Off. Off!" I yelled in desperation.

Ginger began barking in response. Deep bellowing barks. Right. Next. To. My. Ear. The sound echoing through rather painfully. I needed coffee. "Okay, okay, fine, I'm up!" I yelled to the dog.

Groaning, I pushed myself to a sitting position on the floor, as I contemplated my life coach's advice of beginning the day with affirmations. Taking a deep breath, I uttered aloud, because apparently verbalization is key, "Oh what a glorious morning."

One eye peeked open to observe the result which apparently was just Ginger staring back at me with her head cocked to one side. Super cute, but not helping, rolling back onto my knees so I could use them as leverage and grabbing the edge of the bed for support, I staggered to my feet then plodded to the bathroom to clean my teeth and remove dog spit from my face while avoiding looking in the mirror. Gray was beginning to invade my natural blonde and I just didn't need to see that, or the bags under my eyes from lack of sleep, this morning.

Yawning, I padded through the silent house to the kitchen. Even this early in the morning it was sunny and bright. That was one thing I was particular about when purchasing my house, it had to have lots of windows and sunshine. Granted it's not so sunny in the winter but I love to watch the rain and the thunder and lightning. Oddly, Ginger wasn't afraid of the thunder.

Ginger was a gift from me to me to replace my husband, as if you could really do that, but coming home to an eager happy dog was much better than to an empty house and gave me a sense of security. In time we had developed our little routines, although Ginger knows I don't like getting 'kisses'.

Ginger was a dobherd—half Doberman, half Shepherd. If they can make up designer dog names, then so can I. She was such an adorable tiny little puppy but then she grew and grew and kept growing until now she was over 70 pounds of exuberance. Time had tempered her a bit but it would never completely reduce her need to run and jump and lick. It was never my intention to get such a large dog but I needed something and at the time I couldn't bring myself to get anything that resembled a cat in any way. And she had been so small and cute.

I let Ginger out and started the coffee maker to recover from my wineover. See what I did there? Hangover plus wine. Wineover. At my age, I didn't seem to bounce back from a night out like I used to.

As the scent of coffee filled the air I returned to my room and surveyed my closet and its apparel with bleary eyes. Usually I selected office attire unless a call to a client in the rural area required something less dressy. Let's just say that goats and skirts don't mix well.

Nothing was jumping out at me so I just grabbed the first dress my hand touched and a pair of platform wedges because I'm short and they almost put me on eye level with everyone else. Not that I expected to see anyone today.

Why did I feel so down today? I heard the faint beep beep beep as the coffee maker finished and took the opportunity to leave my clothing choices on the bed and returned to the quiet kitchen. I poured the deep brown liquid into my favorite mug and leaned against the granite counter inhaling the aroma. There's something special about drinking out of a favorite mug because it reminds me of a moment in time that I can relive as I hold it in my hands. That, and that I used to have a life. Wow, where did that thought come from?

This particular mug was clay and splashed with multiple colors of reds, oranges and blues mixing into each other. My husband and I bought it on a trip through the Grand Canyon. It reminded me of the hot desert and the cool, endless river. With a deep sigh, I opened the fridge and poured a splash of milk into my coffee.

A deep woof at the kitchen door reminded me I had forgotten about Ginger. Again. Poor baby, she really deserved better. Ugh, every time I drink, I feel like crap the next day. Getting old really sucks.

The open door revealed a disgruntled doggy face. "I know Ginger, mommy's sorry. Let's get breakfast." This information was received with a burst of doggy tail wagging followed by a quick trot to her breakfast bowl where she sat and looked at me with expectation.

Part of me still expected the cat to jump on the counter and meow for food but she was gone too, ten long years, along with my husband. That's why I got Ginger because it would break my heart to get another cat.

After feeding Ginger, I ran some water through the coffee maker to make oatmeal, checking to ensure I had not left the coffee grounds inside. Yeah, coffee oatmeal isn't good. Neither is coffee apple cider or coffee tea but coffee hot cocoa isn't bad. Yeah, I don't always learn the first time.

With food and a couple cups of coffee in me I managed to finally get dressed and out the door. The sun was just beginning to crest the mountains as I pulled my car out of the garage.

The rays of sunlight shining through the pines and back lighting the branches never failed to inspire awe in me. The Sunday paper was lying on the lawn, probably wet as we had a light rain last night. Oh well, maybe it will be dry by the time I get back.

One might ask why I'm headed to church so early but you would be wrong. In fact, I am actually headed to the office. Why? Because it's Sunday and no one will be there and that's the best time to get things done. I bring it on myself because I really listen to people and then they want to talk. Trust me a closed door is no deterrent.

So here I am on a Sunday, driving through the beautiful tree lined streets of Appleby. My home for the last 10 years. I used to live in Morecroft, a town of 150,000 across the lake but I just couldn't stay there. Too many memories, so I ran away, here, to this beautiful small town of just over 15,000 residents where I'm a real estate agent, the toughest job I never wanted.

Things rarely go right in real estate transactions and when they do you still have to deal with temperamental clients and agents. I did have a dream come true once; the agents were awesome, the clients were easy to deal with and the loan went through like a knife through butter. But that was a one in a hundred deal, a unicorn, most of the rest were...messy.

It truly is a beautiful Sunday morning though with the birds singing and a cool, gentle breeze. (See? Positivity.) It almost feels like spring instead of early fall. The rain had left a slight chill in the air which was refreshing. It seems like the rain always makes the colors of the foliage look deeper and brings out the smell of the trees.

I live on the outskirts of town and it takes a good twenty minutes on winding roads through the forest to reach downtown and that's why I chose it, as the drive always relaxes me and improves my mood, and trust me, sometimes I really need it, like today, although for the life of me I couldn't say why I was in such a funk.

My little two bedroom cottage is perfect for me and Ginger. Okay, it's not a cottage, merely a house but cottage has more romantic connotations to it. As a child I always wanted to live in a fairy tale cottage in the forest with roses growing over the front porch, like in the fairy tales, and this is almost it. Perhaps it would be closer to my dream if I actually planted the roses.

The population here varies with the tourists. With the onset of fall and cooler weather, the tourist trade has slowed to a trickle along with the housing market which is one of the reasons why I am going to my office on a quiet Sunday morning. The tourists will pick up come October for Fall Festival but the housing won't until spring.

Still, we get a few snow bunnies, who think the weather is awesome until they can't get to the store or work without a whole lot of shoveling snow and then they sell and move away. Visiting a cute place is a lot different than living here year round and this turnover provides me with a steady business.

AT THE OFFICE

There was another car in the lot this morning as I parked which was unusual for this time of day. Unlike me, most everyone was probably enjoying their Sunday morning at home with family, getting ready for church, but I had some listings to look up before I could go home and enjoy the rest of my Sunday, just me and Ginger watching old black and white movies. I'm sure my friend Vana would frown on the fact that I was skipping church but I just have so much to do. I have to get my bills paid.

The sound of my heels clicking on the polished tile floor echoed around the empty space. It was lonely and peaceful all at the same time. Silence because the office is usually full of conversation as the agents consulted with their clients, is different from silence when no one is expected in. One is pleasant and one is almost creepy. My office was just down the hall and around the corner, conveniently located near the printers and halfway to the bathrooms.

Bathroom location is always important. You don't want to be too close but you don't want to have to traipse a block to get there either, it makes it easier on the clients and myself because, well, I'm getting older.

Unlocking the door I quickly went inside and closed the door behind me and pretended it was quiet because I was earlier than everyone else. Settling behind my glass desk, I flipped open my computer, navigating to our MLS which stands for Multiple Listing Service. It contains every house in town that's available to rent or buy, and I began my search for the perfect home for my buyers.

I've always felt the best part of real estate is being able to make my own schedule. Of course the worst part of being a real estate agent is also making my own schedule. It's the clients really. They seem to think if you're their agent they own you. For the most part though, they are pretty great.

Take the Marples, George and Marilyn, they are real sweethearts. George is a pudgy, balding man in his 70s who worked as a salesman for forty years. He's been married to his wife, Marilyn for 52 years. She reminds me of Betty White, sweet but a little bit feisty. She was your typical housewife, raising the kids and taking care of the home and now they want to retire to Florida. They are selling their single story, 1950s home with no upgrades, because if it was good enough for them, it's good enough for the buyers. They are also not going to do any repairs because, well, you know.

Mmm maybe they're not so sweet. Maybe my assistant Joe is right and I only focus on the good in people but I don't think that's a bad thing, is it? Back to the Marples, they are very pleasant to talk to and have plenty of stories about the history of our town. It will really be a shame when they move because all of that knowledge will be gone with them.

What I'm really working on are listings for my new buyers, Toni and Mora Makimoto, also retirees. They relocated to the United States in the '50s and chose Appleby because it reminded them of their childhood home in Japan. They are looking for a classic with a lot of space for family to visit, with a large kitchen and garden space. Mr. Makimoto likes to cook and grow his own vegetables and herbs. Living in the mountains will allow their children to visit with their families and enjoy the recreation available here year round.

I've narrowed the list down to three — a colonial, a Tudor, and a modern home. If the buyers can't define what they want, and trust me, they can be very vague, then it helps to show them a variety. By finding what they like, or don't like, about a particular house, you can narrow down what they are looking for until you hit the nail on the head. The one caveat is to never really look at more than three homes in a day because buyers develop brain fatigue and mix up details. It's like looking for wedding dresses on those television shows, after too many they end up just walking out the door and not getting a dress, or home. Too many choices.

They'll pick one, I just have a feeling about it and my instinct is pretty good, after all I've been doing this for ten years now. As I continue to look for other possibilities my eye drifts over to the pile of envelopes on the corner of my desk. I've been studiously avoiding them all week but they silently nag at me. Sighing, I reluctantly take my hand off the cursor and sift through them. Bills, bills, bills.

Dwelling on them creates a pit in my stomach that churns as I look through each one that wants money I don't have. People seem to have the perception that real estate agents are successful and rich. The truth is only 20 percent of agents are that successful and I've been there, unfortunately life will happen and success is just as easy to lose. It takes so much hard work to keep a business going and because it's just me, setbacks cause the momentum to falter and any faltering is another deal that doesn't happen.

Don't get me wrong, I love it and wouldn't change a thing but I haven't been generating the income like I should. A sprained knee during the summer didn't help. But I always come through and I will this time too. As long as nothing gets in the way, what are the chances of that happening again?

Okay, well there's no guarantee I won't need surgery or that I won't trip and sprain my ankle but I'm being extra careful these days. What I can't anticipate are buyers suddenly canceling on me or transactions that fall out of escrow and unfortunately it seems like I've had more than my share of those lately. Primarily deals that have Bonnie Belmar on the other side. She just may be the most incompetent agent I've ever worked with.

How she manages to remain one of the top agents in town is beyond me. She moved here just about five years ago and immediately rose to the top but there's something about her that gets on my last nerve. Sometimes it's like she's deliberately trying to bait me, but that's ridiculous right? Plus, everyone else seems to think she's okay.

Resolutely, I put the bills down. I've been on top before and I will be again. I just need to focus on one step at a time and my first step is focusing on the homes I'll be showing Monday and not focusing on Bonnie. Even thinking about her name leaves a bad taste in my mouth. No. The Makimoto's will choose a house and it will close and I will get those bills paid this month.

So my schedule this week is:

Monday

9 am Home inspection at Carol Oates

Tuesday

9 am Show the Makimotos ($500,000) homes

Also

9 am Home inspection at the Marples (Joe handling)

2 pm Show my investor Mark Brown (any good deal) homes in the afternoon.

Wednesday

6 pm Door knocking around the Oates' home

Listing interview with Mr. and Mrs. Hotchkiss ($2.2 million) find a home for Emmeline, a 25 year old momma's girl with no set price. We've already looked at 12 (remember too many homes?)

Thursday
Friday

• • • •

A knock at the door interrupts my planning. A head with dark hair sprinkled with gray poked around the door. Ugh, I didn't lock the door. "Hi Omar, what are you doing in today?" He took a moment to look around the office before responding which always annoyed me. Just who did he expect to catch in here with me?

"Just doing a little catch up and you?"

"Same." I replied with one word because I really don't want to encourage him to stay. Omar is middle aged like me and also single, like me and that's why he implies we should go out. He's tall, dark and fairly good looking with brown eyes but in an icky playboy way. Definitely nothing I would be looking for.

"Oh," he replied hesitantly.

"Did you need something? I'm really busy right now." Please leave, please leave, please leave, I repeated like a mantra.

"Oh, uh, no," he said looking disappointed. "I'll just be over at my desk. You know where it is."

"Yes, I do," I replied politely because I'm polite to everyone. As my mother endlessly repeated, 'polite over impolite is right.' "I'll talk to you later then?"

"Uh, yeah, I'll be here for a while so if you want me to walk you to your car later or...," his voice trailed off expectantly. The machismo is strong with this one.

"Thanks for the offer but I'll be fine, I'm not staying that late." My lip tried to twitch up to a cheer but I managed to hold it down.

"Okay, well if you need me... " his voice trailed off and he walked out without shutting the door which I then quietly shut and locked, thankful he'd left so easily then tried to refocus back on work. A study once found that interruptions cause something like 45 minutes in lost productivity every time they happen. Seems a bit high to me but here I am with my brain now wandering instead of working.

Two hours later Omar interrupted me again. "Yes?" I sighed impatiently as he jiggled the door knob.

"Just wanted to see if you wanted to grab some breakfast?" He yelled through the door.

"No thanks, I'm good," I yelled back. Great, no sound of footsteps leaving. The silence was broken by another question.

"You gonna be okay here by yourself?"

Grrr. What am I two? "Yes, the doors are locked. I'll be fine. Go enjoy your breakfast." Without me. I added mentally. He finally walked away and part of me wanted to jump up and leave while I had the chance in case he came back but the responsible part of me made me stay and finish my work which was interrupted five minutes later by the phone.

This better not be Omar! It wasn't.

"Hey Vana, aren't you supposed to be at church?"

"I just got out. What are you doing? Want to grab lunch?"

"I'm just going over my schedule for the week."

"You're not at the office are you?"

"What? No. I told you I wasn't going in today,"

"Well that's good. I guess that car I'm next to in the parking lot isn't yours then."

Oops, busted. "Okay, I am but just a few things."

"Really cuz we passed your car this morning on the way to church. Two hours ago."

"Fine, yes, I'm working."

"Well get out here I'm hungry and Bob's getting impatient."

I involuntarily snorted a laugh. Bob was the most patient husband you'd ever meet. "Okay, you win. I'm coming out."

I shut down my computer and loaded up my files and headed outside, peeking through the blinds on my door first. Omar didn't appear to be anywhere around as I left which was a relief. It gets tiring constantly shutting someone down and it really irks me when a guy can't take a hint. Not that he'd ever actually asked me out. Just innuendos here and there.

The door clicked shut firmly behind me as I stepped into the sunshine. There's just something about a fall crisp day with the cool breeze and the warm sunshine that just feels so comfortable and pleasant that I can't resist. Closing my eyes, I lifted my face to the sunshine, feeling the warmth and enjoying the scent of fall.

"Come on sun goddess," yelled Vana out the car window.

"Hey Bob, hey Vana," I greeted them. "I'll follow you. Where are we going?"

"To Katie May's. Best breakfast in town." We both said the last sentence in unison and then laughed.

Glancing around the parking lot, I could see that Omar had indeed left.

"Let's go slowpoke," yelled Vana again so I dumped my files in the backseat and followed her out of the parking lot.

KATIE MAY'S FOR BREAKFAST

Katie May's Country Kitchen was located in downtown Appleby and despite numerous other restaurants, was hands down the best for breakfast, lunch or dinner and was relatively inexpensive. Their slogan was 'down home cookin' during the day and winin' and dinin' at night' and they had the best of both. It was also fairly private with booths and divider panels between each. So many restaurants were moving to the open floor plans but here in our little town we still enjoyed being able to have a conversation over food and it was our little group's go to place.

"So I've got you a date for Saturday night," Vana stated as we were seated at a booth with a red checked tablecloth.

"Don't look at me like that. It's about time you started living again." Vana was my coworker but first and foremost, my nearest and dearest friend. She was short like me and plump like me, but was a brunette with a bob and golden brown eyes. I might be a little envious of her eyes. They were just so pretty. Her husband Bob was the total opposite, tall, thin and a lot of facial hair with blue eyes. He was our local postal clerk and knew more people than us real estate agents.

"I live," I responded defensively.

"Yeah, for work. You're always taking care of everyone else, you need someone to take care of you for a change, even if it's just for one night."

Sighing, I said "fine." She was right but I didn't want to admit it. I wasn't ready yet, or maybe I was just afraid, plus Vana's blind dates had a tendency to be, let's just call them quirky. "As long as he isn't a nut case like the last guy that liked to feed the squirrels."

"There's nothing wrong with feeding wildlife," she said defensively with her head buried in the menu.

"There is if they also think they are a squirrel." I argued back.

"She's got you there," jumped in Bob.

Vana bit her bottom lip before commenting, "The one before that wasn't so bad?"

"Oh, you mean the one who got angry when I didn't want to stay home and raise his children? That not so bad one?"

Vana mumbled something from behind the menu she had ducked behind.

"What was that?"

"Okay. I will admit that those two may have been bad choices, but this guy is promising. He doesn't dress up, although he looks really good in a suit, and his kids are grown." As I glared at her, she threw her hands up in the air. "Okay, I promise, if this doesn't work out I will never suggest another date again."

I held my hand out to her across the table. "Pinky swear?"

"Oh fine! I pinky swear," she said as she wrapped her pinky around mine. Her husband looked at her with raised eyebrows. Vana rounded on him.

"Don't say a word." He raised his hands in the air and shook his head.

BABYSITTING DUTY

It's Monday and although I worked yesterday, I love Mondays. It's a fresh start to a new week and new possibilities. Woo hoo, listen to me. That's an affirmation for you. Everybody's in the office raring to go and I look forward to joining them.

I woke before the alarm, and jumped out of bed. Sunlight was just creeping across my floor through the window. I'm going to get so much done today. I've got a home inspection at Carol Oates' farm. She's getting divorced and has a ton of animals so I'll need to dress in boots, jeans and a long sleeved shirt. After getting sneezed on by a goat once I learned. The worst part wasn't that the goat sneezed, no, it was finding the goop later when I stuck my hand in it and realized I'd been walking around with it on my skirt all day. Ugh.

Dressed and fed, I headed to the garage as the phone rang. Honestly, I think talking with Vana and Bob yesterday changed my mood. She just has a way of getting me to see the world differently that makes sense to me and always makes me feel better. Fishing my phone out of my bag, my shoulders tensed as I saw the name.

Swiping to answer I started to say hello when I was cut off by a rush of words. "Hello mom?" I was wondering if you could watch Cassie today, she's got a bit of a fever and I'm late for work."

"Why hello, Penelope," I replied slowly, taking a deep breath and trying to relax my shoulders. "You know you really should let me at least say hello first."

"Hi mom, I'm sorry. It's just that I've got so much to do today and I really can't take off and I didn't want you to say no before I had a chance to explain." There was just a touch of whine in her voice. Penelope is 24 and gorgeous but I think maybe I over indulged her after we lost her father. Making good choices is not her forte which is why she is single with a four year old daughter and automatically assumes I will always be at her beck and call.

I let the silence stretch on for a moment. "Mom?"

"I'm thinking."

"Mom!"

I let out an inaudible sigh. "Just today. I will have to rearrange my meetings and get my assistant to go to the home inspection I had scheduled," I said emphasizing the point that I too had a job. "I want you to understand that I absolutely cannot do it tomorrow. Find someone else to watch her if you need to."

"Just today mom I promise. Thank you so much mom. Bye." She said, clicking off before I could respond. Penelope worked as a graphic designer and her hours were much like mine, but she had recently accepted several new contracts that would, and I quote, "put me on the map."

I was happy for her, really I was, but sometimes I just didn't feel appreciated.

I took a deep breath and blew it out slowly, closed the garage door and rehung my keys. Half of me was happy to drop everything and watch my granddaughter but the other half was frustrated at rearranging my schedule yet again, although I am really good at rearranging. Maybe too good. This watching Chloe was really becoming too frequent. I love my granddaughter but Grandma still needs to work. I still have a mortgage and bills to pay and Penelope needed to understand that. At least I was dressed for grandkid watching.

My assistant Joe is phenomenal. When I phoned him, he assured me he would have everything taken care of after I explained the situation to him and he told me not to worry. I was so lucky to find him. Let's just say I've gone through too many assistants in the past year. Honestly, I'm a good boss and I have no control over accidents. Cheery as usual, I could still hear the judgment in his voice. Joe felt my daughter was taking advantage of my good nature and he might be right but I'd had to leave Penelope so much when I had to go back to work. Watching my granddaughter was just a small way to make up for what I'd had to miss with her. It would never replace the lost time with my daughter, nothing would, but it was the one thing I could do for Penelope now to help her out.

A short 15 minutes later the doorbell rang and my granddaughter Chloe was on the porch. "Nana!" she cried, rushing to give me a big hug over her blankie and teddy bear. Now who wouldn't love that?

"Hello sweetheart. Ginger is waiting for you on the couch and you can both watch your favorite cartoons today." Chanting "Bluey, Bluey," she marched through the door with Ginger on her heels.

Looking up at the toot of a car horn, I saw Penelope waving at me through her open car window. "Gee thanks mom, you're the best. Definitely just this one day," she assured me as she drove off. Knowing she didn't get out of the car because she didn't want a lecture from me, left me feeling a little disgruntled. The porch felt chilly from the morning dew as I grabbed Chloe's backpack off the ground and followed her back inside.

Joe was right. Watching my granddaughter was becoming a too common occurrence. I settled her on the couch, snuggling her blanket around her and Teddy. Ginger snuggled up against her side and went to sleep. Oh, to be a dog without a care in the world.

With the television on in the background, I settled at my kitchen table with my laptop and files. I discovered rather quickly after beginning in real estate that it was easiest just to carry everything around with me. Being mobile was a help and a hindrance and was why my daughter felt she could just drop in whenever.

At 11 am I received a phone call from Carol Oates. It was probably about the home inspection. I like to be there during the inspection so if there are any problems, I can handle it but Joe was also equally as capable, in fact, it was hard to believe that he'd only been with me for six months.

"Hello Caro...,"

"Holly, you have to come help me. I think the police are going to arrest me." Her frantic voice cut in over me.

"Arrest you for what?" I answered as I glanced over to Chloe and Ginger to see if they could hear the phone call. They were both still entranced, Chloe with Bluey and Ginger with sleeping, so I walked into the bedroom and shut the door behind me.

"I, I think they think I killed my husband. They want to know where he is. I told them he was camping but they don't believe me. I told them I didn't do it but they found the pig in the garage and said it looked suspicious."

Carol was a sweet, slightly air-headed woman who loved animals, perhaps a little too much, which is why she had a mini farm up in the hills. She and her husband were currently divorcing which is why I was selling their home for them. I hadn't actually met Jerry in person, just spoke with him over the phone during the listing, which he then signed electronically. This is not an unusual thing to happen if one party is out of the area.

"Why would a pig be suspicious? You have a farm. Wait...where's the pig," I asked hoping I had misheard because she had a home inspection this morning.

"Well it was dead, so I fed it to the dogs. Now they think I fed him to the pigs. You have to help me," she wailed.

"Wait, what?! Back up a minute. The pig in your garage is DEAD? And why were the dogs eating it? Didn't the home inspector come this morning?

"Yes, he came but he left already."

"Did he see the pig?"

"Ummm. I think the important point is the police," she demurred.

I realized I was smacking my forehead with my palm and made myself stop. I could figure this out. I had to if I was going to close this deal.

"Where's Joe?"

"Joe?"

"My assistant. He was supposed to be there for the home inspection."

"Oh, yeah, Joe, he was here and then he left with the inspector."

Why would he leave with the inspector? "Carol. Where is the inspector?"

"Oh well he's with Joe," she replied as if that was the most obvious thing in the world. As I said, Carol wasn't the brightest banana in the bunch.

I could feel my frustration rising as this conversation went in circles. "And where are Joe and the inspector?"

"Oh well, they're both in the back yard with the police," she stated matter of factly.

Taking a deep breath, I began again. "Carol, are the police arresting you right now?"

"Well, no, they just told me not to leave town and I might want to call a lawyer."

"That's a great idea, Carol, you should do that. Call your lawyer and I'll talk to Joe and find out what the police know. I'm sure this is just a simple misunderstanding."

"Are you sure? Because I'm really scared right now. What if something did happen to Jerry?"

"Listen Carol, just call your lawyer and let's wait until we have more news," I said in as comforting a tone as possible when a thought struck me. "Um, why are the police in the backyard if the pig is in the garage?"

"Because of the bones that got washed into the neighbor's yard."

"What bones Carol?" My voice may have been just a touch harsh.

She hemmed and hawed for a few minutes then finally confessed. "I bury my dead animals in the backyard. Everybody does and it wouldn't have been a problem if the pipes weren't so close to the surface. I told Mike not to drive over them but does he ever listen to me? No. It's because I'm a woman."

I released the breath I had been holding during this monologue out through my lips. "You never disclosed any of this information to me. This might be an issue for the buyers and now I've got to do an addendum."

"Do you really? Everybody does it," she whined. "And what about the police?"

Swallowing my frustration with her, I put a smile on my face before speaking. People can tell if you're smiling when talking over the phone. "Listen Carol, I'll take care of the disclosure and talk to Joe. You call your lawyer and try to reach Jerry. You can't be arrested if he's alive."

I heard a deep sigh on the phone and then,"Okay, you're right. I'll call the lawyer and keep trying to reach Jerry. Are you coming over?"

"I can't right now, I've got my granddaughter with me but Joe is there and he's perfectly capable. Listen, I'll come over tomorrow and we'll figure this out."

"Thanks Holly, I don't know what I'd do without you," she added with a sob.

My phone beeped. "I'm getting another call, I'll talk to you tomorrow and we'll sort this out. Just stay strong." I clicked over to the other call before receiving an answer.. "Hello Joe."

"Um, not sure where to start on this one," he replied.

"Just start at the beginning. It's about Carol right?" I could hear him take a deep breath and blow it out on the other end of the phone.

"Yes. I showed up and the inspector was already here. He was nearly done when we found the mess in the garage. He was really nice but he said there was no way he was putting that in his report. He said he would call to reschedule. Such a nice man," he added.

I groaned inwardly. This would set things back and probably necessitate a reinspection fee which Carol would pay without complaint. "And the police?" I prompted.

"Yeah that." There was a long pause and then, "She hasn't been arrested but the police said she can't leave town. Apparently they found Jerry's body in his house Monday morning."

"He's dead?" I questioned, shocked. "But Carol said the police can't find him. Are you sure he's dead? Why wouldn't they tell Carol that?"

There was a long pause, "Joe, you still there?"

"Uh, yeah, I was just thinking. My friend said they found his body, maybe she made a mistake."

"Well, you should keep that information to yourself until you find out for sure," I admonished him. "No sense in stressing out Carol more than she already is."

"Of, course. I'll try and find out for sure," he said apologetically.

"Okay, thank you Joe, if you hear anything else please keep me informed and please reassure Carol."

I sat on my bed to think. Why hadn't the police told Carol her husband was dead if he was dead? This created a huge problem because the death of a party to a transaction immediately canceled the transaction. You're probably thinking that this is kind of callous of me but the fact is, I'm a real estate agent and despite the tragedy, I have to think of all the other parties involved. Plus, I've had my share of tragedy. You just have to move on if you want to survive.

Now seemed like a great time for a break. I walked back out to the living room and evicted Ginger from the couch (seriously she takes up the whole thing) and snuggled next to Chloe to watch "Bluey" with her. At least for the next few hours this was exactly what I needed to be doing. Besides, it was the episode with the grannies on the bus and it was hilarious.

DREADFUL DELAYS

Tuesday dawned bright and clear, no rain, no clouds which is good because I have a lot to do today and storms can come up suddenly here in the mountains. The sun stretched all the way across the bedroom floor when I woke up. My sleeping had been disturbed by visions of home inspectors and dead pigs.

Breakfast was a hurried affair with instant oatmeal and coffee. Dressing quickly, I let Ginger out to use the backyard facilities, then filled her food and water dishes. It was a nice enough day, so I left the doggy door open for her. Grabbing my keys and purse, I opened the garage door and paused. Nope, no phone ringing. Tip toeing through I shut it quietly behind me and got in my car.

Yes! No phone calls, no kids to watch, no emergencies, well other than Carol who I was going to see right after my 9 a.m. showings with the Makimotos. It would make a tight schedule but as long as everything went smoothly I should be fine. I put the key in the ignition and was greeted with Click, click, click.

"What the heck?" I sagged against the steering wheel, sighing deeply. Taking a calming breath, I fished out my phone and called a tow company which assured me they would be there within 20 minutes. I guess my day isn't looking as bad as I thought it was, I was totally expecting an hour or longer wait.

True to their word, and much to my surprise, the tow truck driver was pulling up 20 minutes later. He was a heavy set, kind looking man, with a shock of dark hair. He was probably really handsome back in the day. At close to six feet, he towered over me.

"Well ma'am it looks like your battery is dead." The tow truck driver pushed his hat up on his forehead as he stepped back from the engine. He wiped his hands on a rag as he explained, "This happens a lot when the weather changes. Soon as there's a cold snap, pffht," he snapped his fingers, "that's it, dead. I recommend you get another one as this one isn't going to hold a charge if you drive with your lights on. Might start again during the day but I wouldn't take the chance. I brought one with me just in case."

"But my car drove fine when I came home yesterday."

"Well, it will. In fact you can actually drive a car without a battery in it once it's started. But if you stop the engine and the battery is bad, it won't start again."

"Well, thank you, Mister..."

"Belroy ma'am, Amos Belroy. Thank you for asking. Most folks nowadays don't want to get to know a person. You know what I mean?" Amos paused his stream of words and pushed back the baseball cap on his head.

"Yes, I do, Amos. It seems to be a long lost courtesy nowadays. Well, I guess I'm getting a new battery so I'll take the one you have because I really do need to get into the office today and I have a busy week."

"Sure thing, ma'am. I'll get that installed right away."

"Do you have to rescue people in their driveways often?"

"More often than you might think. Heck just this weekend I had to pull a truck out of a field. Owner was working with the lights on and ran the battery down. A lot of times it's because the cables are loose, thought that was the case this time but no, the battery was really dead. Too bad, because it was a fairly new one.

"Excuse me," I said as my phone rang. The morning breeze was chilly as I stepped out of the garage to see it was my assistant Joe calling. I pressed the button to answer, "hello Joe, what's up?"

I could hear Joe sigh before he said, "Bonnie called and she said they had to reschedule again. I'm really sorry, I didn't know what to say."

"It's okay, Joe. I'll handle it," I replied and disconnected. I could feel my anger beginning to rise as I watched the tow truck driver working on my car. His hat was cockeyed and his gray overalls were already filthy with grease and grime. This was the second time Bonnie had "rescheduled" the home inspection and I was beginning to feel it was a delaying tactic. We had a 30 day escrow and were already three weeks in. Oh, she always had a reasonable excuse but it was more likely her client's financing was falling apart which is not my client's problem.

Ten minutes later, I was backing the car out of the garage and heading to the office. Amos was a real sweetheart, insisting on making sure everything was cleaned up before shutting the hood. He waited while I started the car before heading on to his next job.

I tried to let my zen drive calm me but today it wasn't working, so instead of turning in at my office, I drove past it to Balmar Realty and pulled into the parking lot. Her office was in the older part of town and was a former house converted to a business.

Every time I had a deal with Bonnie on the other side, there was some sort of problem and unfortunately, in this small town, she somehow managed to get more than her fair share of buyers and sellers so I was stuck dealing with her. Getting out of my car I tugged my jacket straight and pushed the handle of my purse onto my shoulder then marched briskly into Bonnie's office. Pulled the Notice of Buyer to Perform, I had prepared the other day, out of my bag and laid it on her desk because I suspected this might happen.

"I need the home inspection asap and if you delay any longer we are going to cancel," I declared in a firm voice, well as firm as I could be. This type of behavior was not me. I'm a people pleaser and confrontation always takes an extra effort on my part.

Bonnie pursed her lips and squinted her eyes at me not bothering to pick up the paper. In her late 50's she had a tendency to color her hair an unnatural red which only accentuated the perpetual smug look on her slightly pudgy face. Bonnie had been a thorn in my side since she got her broker's license and sold her first million dollar house. Now she thought she was better than the rest of us and I think it irked her that we, the other realtors, didn't care. She'd only been in town for five years but for some reason, she particularly didn't like me. I try to be nice to everyone but she really stretches my patience.

"I can't help it if the inspector is busy, Holly," she replied in a sickeningly sweet voice. She sat behind her desk with her hands clasped together on top.

Not feeling it, I smiled back at her. "If I call the inspector will he say the same thing?" I added in my own sweet voice. Bonnie's eyes flared slightly back at me, confirming my suspicions she was stalling. "I'm sure, you're doing your best, but my clients need to get their house sold so please inform the inspector that you'll have to get a new one if he can't make it. You've got three days," I added as I walked out the door not waiting for her reply. I've found that confrontations are always easier if you have facts on your side and thankfully, the state real estate association had our backs covered.

Back in my car and headed toward my office, I soothed myself by focusing on my upcoming appointments. I'm a planner and I like to have a schedule as it keeps me on time and focused on my job. Well, that's the lie I tell myself. I'm late to everything. Seriously, I don't know anyone in my field who is actually on time, there's always an unspoken 'ish' added to it.

This morning I had my showing appointments with the Makimotos and an investor and of course talking to Carol. What in the world was she thinking dragging a dead pig in the garage when she had a home inspection scheduled? My thoughts were quickly tempered by the thought that her soon to be ex might be dead. Why hadn't the police told her he was dead? If he was. Maybe Joe got it wrong somehow. I would have to ask. It should be fairly easy to find someone camping. On an impulse I made a phone call.

"Appleby Police Department," said a female voice as my call went through.

"Hi, my name is Holly Holcraft and I'm a real estate agent working with Carol Oates. The police were just at her house yesterday and I heard her husband died? Is there someone that could confirm that?" I asked.

I was immediately asked to hold and suffered through several minutes of elevator hold music from the 70's. Couldn't they get something more updated to listen to?

"Hello, this is Detective Moran, you have information about the Oates?" he asked abruptly in a deep voice..

"Well, no, I was inquiring if Jerry was in fact dead because it would affect the sale of their house."

"I can't give you information on a pending case." The smugness just oozed through the phone.

"I just need to know if he is in fact deceased."

"Did the wife tell you he was dead?"

I held the phone away from my ear and looked at it. Was I not speaking clearly? "No she did not," I enunciated each word clearly. "Is. He. Dead? Is anyone dead?"

"I can't say. Look if you don't have any pertinent information, I'm busy. Call me back if you know anything." The phone clicked off.

Grrr, this was so frustrating! I was about to put my phone away when I heard a whisper on the line.

"Hello?" I said.

"Is this Holly?"

"Yes, it is. Who is this?"

"It's me Penny, you sold my mom a house last year. Moran is a jerk," she whispered into the phone. "I shouldn't tell you this but they did find a body in Mr. Oates' apartment... Uh oh someone's coming I've gotta go." The line went dead.

Well, that didn't help. Maybe it wasn't Jerry. If I just knew. I wanted to scream with frustration. He could really be camping like Carol said. It didn't make sense she would kill him. It was an amicable divorce. Well Carol said it was and Jerry hadn't said otherwise. He was supposed to sign escrow docs soon, so I crossed my fingers that he showed up except, who died in Jerry's house? If it wasn't Jerry, it wouldn't affect the transaction but it's always tragic when there's a death and it must have been someone he knew. I would have to get a sympathy card ready for him and did Carol know the person? Maybe not, she thought it was Jerry that died but then why wasn't she arrested? Ugh, I'm just thinking in circles now. Focus on one thing at a time Holly!

SHENANIGANS

Hours later I walked through my front door in a daze, dropping my keys and purse on the table before plopping on the couch. This really had been the worst day ever. If I had ever imagined a worse day than this when I began my real estate career 20 years ago, I would never have started.

Not that I had much choice at the time. As a single mom with a kid, there just wasn't much choice. It was either this or wait tables and I've always been pretty clumsy, so real estate agent it was.

Ginger jumped up next to me and began sniffing me thoroughly as a horrible smell reached my nose. I sniffed my blouse then gagged. It was me! Argh the smell from the house I showed to the investor earlier had traveled home with me. Thankfully, it was after the Makimoto showings. I pushed Ginger away and dashed to the bathroom. I pulled my clothes off, careful not to let them come in contact with my face anymore than was absolutely necessary.

In the shower I pressed my hands against the wall and leaned into the hot spray of the water, then proceeded to wash my hair three times but I swore I could still smell the cat urine and God only knows what other creatures had infested the carpet and walls in the foreclosure house as I toweled off. How the investor could stand the smell I will never know but he took FOREVER to leave. I would have been out the door, well actually, I wouldn't have gone inside if I didn't have to. Maybe the lure of money was more provocative than the smell was disgusting.

And that was after the Makimoto debacle.

I met them in front of a beautiful two-story Tudor. Toni and Mori Makimoto, the older couple who need room for kids to visit with their grandchildren. They are in their late 60's and they both wear a perpetual smile.

The Tudor is truly beautiful and the landscaping is perfect and I just knew this was going to be a quick in and out and then I could, as they say, seal the deal and we wouldn't even have to see the other two homes.

"You are going to love this house," I said to them. "It has everything you want including a workout room. The sellers are moving to Florida to retire," I continued as I opened the front door. The sellers were both at work but I called out anyway. "Hello! Real estate agent. Anyone home?" Receiving no answer we all proceeded into the stone entryway.

"That will be wonderful," said the wife, Toni. "My husband and I have been wanting to create our own spa retreat so a workout room will be perfect.

"I just love the Tudor style," she continued, "especially the leaded glass windows. They always look so cozy and the grandkids are going to love it too. It will be just like living in one of those English cottages they read about all the time."

Her husband just nodded his head in agreement and followed his wife down the hall.

This Tudor was a four bathroom, five bedroom home with 3,175 square feet of space. A beautiful house and an equally awesome commission. I really needed to close this deal. With fingers crossed we proceeded to the kitchen first because that is one of the major selling points of any house.

This kitchen was located smack in the center of the house with the living room, and dining areas opening off of it which was the major reason the Makimoto's wanted it.

"This kitchen is huge with a great pantry and they just installed new lighting including under cabinet lights. What do you think Mr. Makimoto? Your wife said you love to cook," I inquired.

"This place is spectacular. I think we will be very happy here and it's going to be perfect when the family visits," he paused and cocked his head to the side. "What is that noise?"

I stopped to listen and could hear a regular thump thump thump. "That's strange, it sounds like someone's on the treadmill but Mr. Hajari said he wouldn't be home today."

"Is it normal for people to be home when you show their houses?" inquired Toni.

"Well people do change their plans," I replied, "but they are the nicest couple and they said buyers were welcome anytime." Explaining as I walked I led the way back down the hallway to the workout room which was where the noise was definitely coming from.

"Mr. Hajari," I raised my voice as we approached the door, "are you in here?" Not receiving any answer, I opened the door.

Mr. Hajari was definitely in the room, on the treadmill and he was definitely not expecting company as he was running on the treadmill naked as the day he was born. Any words I had froze in my open mouth, I watched in shock as his parts bounced unrestrained through the air. For a moment we were all frozen in time when I heard Mrs. Makimoto gasp and I flung my arms to either side to shield their eyes from the sight.

For a moment nothing happened. Then it felt like slow motion but in reality was impossibly quick. Mr. Hajari glanced our way, saw intruders and stopped in shock but, unfortunately the treadmill did not, and half a second later he was tumbled backwards off the treadmill and landing in a heap against the wall. More unfortunate, he landed bottom side up exposing everything for the world to see.

Instinctively I began to shove the Makimoto's backwards toward the door. I turned around and came face to face with their shocked faces. Pushing them both back out the door I yelled over my shoulder, "So, so, so sorry Mr. Hajari. Are you okay? I'll come right back to check on you."

On the other side of the now closed door, I took a deep breath and took a moment to straighten my clothes and regain my composure. Of all the bad luck. I mean things like this happen all the time but not today. Not now. I really needed this deal. Smiling over the twisting in my gut I said, "sometimes these things happen. Why don't you wait outside and I'll just go check and make sure he's okay."

The Makimoto's nodded their heads and slowly walked down the hall with a bewildered look on their faces, the perpetual smile absent. Mr. Makimoto made as if to speak but then closed his mouth and nodded again.

"Mr Hajari," I called through the closed door. "I'm coming in." My query was met with silence so with my heart racing I turned the knob and opened the door just enough to get my head in facing away from the scene of destruction, of course.

"Mr. Hajari, are you okay? Do you need medical help?"

"Mmphh," I was greeted with a muffled voice followed by "no, no! I'm quite all right."

"That's very good Mr. Hajari. I'm going to need you to put some clothes on," I said waving my hand in the general direction of his appendages while averting my eyes. "I'm going to make sure the Makimoto's are okay and then I'll come back to make sure you're alright."

Turning to find what I hoped were still my clients, I found the Makimoto's had retreated to the front lawn.

"That was...that was," began Mori when his wife caught his eye and burst out in laughter.

"Oh my, yes it was," she giggled.

Toni turned to me. "We love the house but we're really going to have to think about it.

"I must agree with my wife," added Mr. Makimoto. "The...atmosphere of the house...we just need to feel things out. You understand right?"

The queasiness in my stomach was increasing but I put a smile on my face and a forced cheerfulness I hoped they didn't notice. "Of course, I understand. This image is something that will take a bit of time to get out of my head."

"You're disappointed," commented Mrs. Makimoto.

"I am but it's because I really felt this was the perfect home for you. I'm just disappointed that this experience has soured the house for you."

"And we really appreciate that," she added. "It's why we chose you in the first place. Now why don't we go take a look at those other two homes?"

INSPECTION EXPECTATIONS

In a subdued mood two houses later, I stopped by the store on my way home to grab a few things before my next appointment at 2 p.m.

Okay, I'll admit it, my weakness is mini powdered sugar donuts. You know the little ones that come in a six pack. As I stood in line at the checkout the cashier, who knows me well, set the package on the little counter where you slide your card. I mean, hey, they were right there in my face. What was I supposed to do? So I popped one in my mouth and it was sooo delicious.

"You really don't need that. Keep eating those and you'll look like that tow truck driver."

"Excuse me?" I directed to the woman standing next to me in line feeling maybe I had misunderstood. She was tall with shoulder length blonde hair and looked to be in her late sixties.

"Those donuts. A woman of your size, you really don't need those. The smugness just oozed out of her. The irony of her statement was apparently lost on the woman as her clothes were themselves a little snug.

I'm sorry what does that have to do with a tow truck driver?

Because he's fat like you," she spat back. "Tromping around in the mud at my neighbors house. He looked like a pig in the mud. People really should be watching their health if they want to keep doing their jobs."

"Wow, you must be having a really bad day," I replied carefully, removing another donut which I slowly popped in my mouth while not losing eye contact with her. I then slowly offered the donuts in her direction.

Not expecting that her mouth dropped open. "Well I, well I..." she stuttered as the others in line tried to stifle their laughter.

"Well okay, then," I replied, gathering my bags. "Everyone has different tastes." The cashier was struggling not to laugh out loud as I walked out through the store doors and high fived the security guard on my way. Sarcastic sass, that was my weapon of choice.

Shower fresh, Ginger wasn't so excited to sniff me anymore. She was even less excited when I gave her a bath and spritzed the couch with air freshener just in case the odor was transferable. Then us two gals retired to the bed wrapped in towels and with some snacks to relax for a few minutes and give our hair a chance to dry.

Ginger was a little miffed when I put down her cracker to answer the phone.

"Hello Vana. Please tell me this is a social call and not work," I begged.

"Rough day?" she laughed.

"You could say that."

"Well this will make you feel better. The girls and I are just running out to get a bite to eat and maybe a drink. Oh what am I saying. We're getting a bottle of wine or two, maybe three and possibly also having a bite to eat. You should come with us. In fact, I'll be there in 15 minutes to pick you up."

"I don't know if I feel up to it."

"What are you going to do? Sit there and mope? You can do it with us instead. It'll be better for you. I'm on my way," she ended and disconnected the call so I couldn't refuse.

Left to my own devices, I grabbed a glass of wine and thought back over my conversation with Carol earlier today as I looked for clothes.

The house had been a mess, and the garage, oh my word, I can't even describe it. Except for the fact that she was deeply in debt and desperately needed this sale to go through, one would think she was trying to sabotage the sale of the house.

"Okay Carol, start from the beginning." I was sitting inside her ranch house on her sofa while she arranged herself on a chair. Her clothing was all disheveled and covered in what looked like dried mud. Which, probably was in fact dried mud, as I noticed a trail leading from the door to her chair.

"The police came to question me because the neighbor found bones in their yard and they haven't seen my husband in a while," she rushed with all the words tumbling over each other.

I took a deep breath. "Let's start at the beginning. I know you said you are getting divorced, where is your husband."

"I told you he went on a camping trip."

"Why didn't you mention this before?"

"See? You don't believe me either," she wailed, waving her hands in all directions.

"Take a deep breath Carol. I don't know what to believe right now. You told me your husband was going to be in town to sign the papers."

"And he will be. He just went camping for a few days. He does this all the time to de-stress. In fact it's one of the reasons we're getting divorced. He has a habit of leaving when things are tough and I have to handle everything."

"Okay," I responded, pursing my lips in frustration. "Never mind that right now. Why are you accused of killing him?"

"Because no one can reach him. He isn't answering his phone." Her breathing was increasing and I could sense hysterics about to start. Tear stains tracked down her face.

I snapped my fingers in front of her face to get her attention, and when that didn't work grabbed her waving hands and placed them in her lap with mine over them. I began again.

"Carol! I really need you to focus on me. Look at my face. Okay? Deep breath. Okay, let's start again. Why," I began slowly, "do the police think something happened to your husband?"

Taking a deep breath and sitting up straight she began, "some bones got washed into my neighbor's yard."

"And?" I prompted.

"They are just animal bones, honest. I bury my dead animals out there."

"Yes, you said that. In the field," I repeated as she nodded in confirmation. "How did they get washed into your neighbors yard?

"Oh yeah," she said as if she had forgotten. "Silly I'm so sorry. A pipe broke in the yard and whoosh everything is now in the neighbor's yard."

"But they're just animal bones right? So everything will be fine," I added looking at her. "They are just animal bones right?"

"Ye, yeah. Yeah."

Something in her response left me feeling a little unsettled.

"And the pig?"

"What else was I going to do with it? I couldn't just leave it outside. I explained it to the inspector, I'm sure he understood."

Well show me the garage so I can see how bad the damage is. Rising reluctantly, she led me to the garage. My phone rang as I stepped into the garage. It was the inspector. "Uh, huh. Well thank you sir. I really, really appreciate that."

I rang off and faced Carol who clearly knew what I was going to say by the sheepish look on her face. "The inspector said he's going to have to come back out again. You didn't tell me he refused to complete the inspection," I said furiously, deciding not to let her know I already knew. This whole thing was going to set us back several days. "You should be grateful he's not charging us again because you would have to pay for it."

Looking around at the mess in the garage, I really was grateful that he was so understanding. There was blood and goop everywhere and it was all I could do not to puke right there. Thankfully, the door was open because the smell was horrendous and I pulled my shirt over my nose to try and block out the odor.

"You need to clean this up right now.

"But,"

"No, right now. Do you want to sell this house or not?" I questioned her. "Seriously, you can't let the buyer's or the agent see this mess. It's bad enough I have to tell them."

"Do you really?" she questioned apprehensively.

Are you kidding me right now? "Yes. If I don't, the inspector will, so spend all night if you have to but clean this mess up. Now."

I just shook my head as I looked around. As I pulled my keys out of my bag they slipped out of my hand onto the grimy floor, then I accidentally kicked them against the wall as I went to pick them up. Age was making me clumsy among other things.

Carol was still heading for the garage door as I picked up my keys and slipped them back into my pocket.

"I'll call you later to see how you're doing." As I turned to leave I smacked my shin and nearly fell over an antique claw foot tub. I pussyfooted my way around the tub making a less than graceful exit.

At the curb I was accosted by Jacob again. This time he was dressed in a track outfit and jogging in place. "Holly. I was wondering if you had a chance to think about my offer?"

Talk about not taking no for an answer. Sighing mentally, I replied. "Jacob, I'm sorry but the house is not available right now. Maybe after escrow closes, the new owners will sell to you."

Jacob stopped jogging and planted his feet, putting his hands on his hips. "Look, I saw all the police out here the other day. I live around the corner. My lawyer told me that if Jerry is dead then the deal is invalidated. So I can buy the house."

"What makes you think Jerry is dead?" I asked dumbfounded.

He shrugged his shoulders. "Simple conclusion. Why else would the police be out here?"

"Well Jerry is not dead. So there's nothing to talk about. I'm sorry but I really need to get to work right now." I walked quickly to my car, locking the doors once inside.

"Okay, just let me know when I can buy it." He yelled after me. He stood in the middle of the road and stared at me as I drove off.

As promised Vana picked me up 15 minutes later.

"Well you look a fright," she commented. Vana Dago was always honest to a fault. She grabbed my suit jacket from the stand by the door. Better not wear this one, it stinks. I'll just put it in the laundry room.

"Oh, wait," I said. "My keys are in the pocket." She put her hand into the jacket pocket and pulled it back out quickly. "Yuck! What the hell is that?" she added as she dropped something goopy on the floor.

She and I both stared at the oblong object on the floor for a moment.

"Is that a...finger bone?"

I pursed my lips together. Where had that come from?

"I don't know. I dropped my keys on Carol's garage floor in all the muck. It must have gotten caught in them."

"Did she kill someone in her garage?" Her eyebrows reached up to her hairline.

"Funny you should ask that." Her comment got me thinking, did she? "She said it was a pig that had died and she was feeding it to her dogs so it wouldn't go to waste." Vana's eyes were as big as saucers as she stared at me.

"She had a dead pig in her garage?"

Raising my eyebrows and nodding my head, I said, "Oh, but it gets better." I quickly filled her in on the highlights of the Carol incident.

"Did they arrest her? Wait. If she was accused of murder why wasn't the garage taped off?"

"Huh." She had me stumped there. "Also, why didn't they tell Carol her husband was dead?"

"Are you kidding me right now?" She replied dumbfounded.

"No. She thinks he's just missing. But Joe said his friend told him they found his body," I paused to think. Carol said the police came because a neighbor found bones in their yard. Is Jerry even dead? "Penny at the police station said they found a body in his house but then she had to leave before I could get anymore information and the detective in charge seems like a jerk," I said, recalling his unpleasant attitude.

"Something doesn't sound right. You said this bone was in her garage. What bones were in the neighbor's yard? Wait." She added holding up her index finger. "We can talk about this when we meet up with the girls. This sounds like a conversation that needs to be accompanied by alcohol. I see you've already started," she said, noting my empty wine glass. I just shrugged my shoulders at her.

Taking my wine glass into the kitchen she grabbed a sandwich bag and encased the bone in it. "I've got a client that works in a crime lab," she said as I raised my eyebrows at her.

Within 30 minutes we were safely ensconced in a booth at Katie May's with Lucy and Shelby.

Vana bringing a tray and four glasses of wine. "I took the liberty of helping myself. Katie doesn't mind," she said, referring to the owner of the place. Her name wasn't really Katie but when she bought the restaurant, everyone just started calling her that and it stuck, actually, I don't even know her real name.

"You just get what ya'll need," Katie yelled over to us in a southern drawl. She's not southern either. "We can settle later. I know ya'll 'er good for it."

"Now tell us all what's going on," cut in Shelby. "Vana said you had a mystery going on."

I looked at Vana.

"What?" she questioned. "I may have texted them while you were getting another jacket, which looks great on you, I might add."

"Flattery will get you everywhere. You sneak." I filled the girls in on the Carol shenanigans leaving out the bit about the bone.

"You know what you need?" began Lucy as I groaned, here it comes. "You need a date. No hear me out," she added as I began to interrupt. This was a regular routine with Lucy who thought sex solved everything. "You spend entirely too much time with real estate. You need a day off once in a while."

"I just had a day off yesterday, with my granddaughter," I began.

"Watching Chloe unexpectedly because your daughter doesn't have a babysitter doesn't count as a day off," added Shelby.

Vana thankfully intervened. "Hey what happened with the Makimoto's?"

My face flushed red as I recounted the incident with Mr. Hajari and the treadmill. The ladies laughed so hard they almost cried.

"Oh my, almost wish I'd been there," gasped Lucy before dissolving into another fit of laughter. Between the wine and the laughter I felt my tensions begin to melt away.

"Well, they said they would let me know, so fingers crossed," I added holding both hands up with my fingers crossed. All the ladies held theirs up as well in solidarity.

"Well things aren't so bad," I added. "My inspector is buying the smelly house. So there's that."

"Thank God, investors don't get home inspections. At least you won't have to go back there until it closes," Shelby said as she pinched her nose with her fingers.

"Cheers to that," said Vana as she raised her wine glass and we all clinked our glasses together with a loud 'cheers.'

Sometime later a loud voice yelled out, "Hey turn up the tv." We all glanced at the television in the corner. A news report was on with a picture of a tow truck driver. "Amos Belroy died in a tragic accident this afternoon when his brakes failed and he suffered a fatal heart attack. Mr. Belroy was well known in the community..." The voice droned on but I was no longer listening.

"Holly, what's wrong?" asked Lucy.

"That's the tow truck driver who helped me this morning. He was so sweet. I can't believe he's dead."

"How ironic is that, a tow truck driver whose brakes failed," commented Shelby shaking her head.

"Really, Shelby, Really?" hissed Lucy.

"I don't think now is the time for that," added Vana raising her glass. "A toast to Mr. Belroy, may he rest in peace."

We said our goodbyes a little after 9 p.m.

Vana drove me home but as I was opening the door she put her hand on my arm. "You didn't say anything about the bone."

I looked at her and shook my head. "It just didn't seem right. Maybe it's best if we don't mention it?"

"Agreed. I'll have my client check it out and let you know what it really is.

BONNIE

Bonnie seethed with anger, her entire body shaking. "That, that woman!" She sputtered. Anger wouldn't begin to describe what she felt for her. She slammed the dishes into the sink. If she broke one and cut herself, it would be Holly's fault. Watching her with her friends, having fun and enjoying herself. She had no right!

The only reason Bonnie had gotten into real estate was to put Holly in her place. After what she had done, she had no right to be successful and cute, although she was beginning to put on a little weight and every pound she gained only made Bonnie happier. Sometimes it's the little things you have to focus on to get you through the day. A smile wreathed her face as she thought about her plan.

Once her friend came through for her, she would have Holly's business also. It was her goal in life to steal every prime listing so that Holly would be forced to deal with her. Slowing down her transactions would certainly inconvenience her. Money wasn't an issue for Bonnie as she was set for life. She didn't have to work if she didn't want to, in fact, the only reason she was working was to make Holly unsuccessful.

Unfortunately, she wasn't doing so well in that aspect and that just made her angrier.

Reaching for her phone, she dialed a number. "Hello," she purred. "I've got another job for you."

DOOR KNOCKING

It seemed like my head barely hit the pillow and I was already waking up. Today was my least favorite part of selling real estate - door knocking. Sometimes it really paid off though, especially in a small town where everybody knows everybody else. It was another day but all the trouble with yesterday and the death of Amos had put a damper on my enthusiasm.

I was meeting with Mr. and Mrs. Hotchkiss later this evening to interview for their listing. They had a beautiful old country house located on the outskirts of town that was easily worth a couple million but I had no doubts about my ability to convince them to list with me. First though, I needed to try and generate some new business, hence the door knocking.

Because I'd just gotten Carol's house into escrow, I decided to door knock around her house.

My heart wasn't in it but it was on my schedule and I liked to keep to my schedule. The house to the left of Carol's was a tidy little single story that had seen better days. It was just little things that made it seem worn like the trim needed painting and the front yard was mostly crabgrass.

An elderly woman came to the door at my knock. She was thin as a rail and had short curly gray hair.

"Hi, I'm Holly and I'm selling your neighbor's house next door," I said cheerily.

Her demeanor immediately put a damper on my enthusiasm.

"What do you want?"

"I'm Ho...," I began again but she cut me off.

"I don't care who you are and tell Mike to stop shining those lights at night it disturbs my cows."

"Tell who, what?" I said in confusion.

"Is there something wrong with your hearing? I said, tell that no good neighbor of mine to stop shining lights in my backyard. It puts my cows off their feed, you know."

"No, I'm sorry I didn't know that. I don't actually live in the neighborhood, I'm just selling Carol Oates's house next door but if your neighbor's home, I can mention it to them when I go over there?"

She looked me over suspiciously. "Why would you do that? You don't know him." She was beginning to frustrate me.

"Just trying to be neighborly," I replied with a smile. "What did you say your name was?"

"I didn't say," she snapped, "but it's Betty, Betty Balmar."

"Balmar? Are you related to Bonnie?"

"That no good for nothing...if you're a friend of hers, I'm done talking," she said and started to close the door.

"Oh no, no," I interjected quickly. "I sometimes have to do business with her but we are definitely not friends." I shook my head to emphasize the point.

"Well, that's good to know." She paused before adding grumpily, "why don't you come in for a spell. I could talk to you for a few minutes but I don't want to be standing at the front door the whole time. I'm old, you know." Her back and forth was giving me mental whiplash.

Plastering a smile on my face I said, "Sure," hoping she wasn't secretly a murderer.

She led me into a cheery yellow kitchen with a blue checkered cloth on the table. Pulling out a wooden chair she indicated for me to sit down.

"Do you like tea?" she inquired.

"Yes, that would be lovely," I said because the best way to break the ice is to share food.

I sat quietly waiting for her to speak and when she didn't I said. "You have a lovely home, Betty, it feels very cozy."

"That's good of you to say but I know it's old and out of date."

"Not at all. It reminds me of my grandma's house and baking cookies," I replied with a smile. I could see a little corner of her mouth quirking up.

"Yes, well I do my best. It's not easy getting older and I've got the cows to take care of since my husband passed on. Betsy and Boris. He raised them from calves.

"I'm sorry to hear that. You mentioned the cows were being bothered at night..." I paused expectantly.

Betty set two fine china cups and saucers on the table and poured the steaming tea into the delicate cups. "My husband brought these over to me from Japan during the war. He was in the service, you know."

"They are beautiful," I added wondering where this conversation was going.

"My Albert, he would never have put up with that young whipper snapper and all his goings on. No, he would have marched right over there and set him straight," she stated perfunctorily with a set jaw as she settled into her chair.

"What sorts of goings on," I inquired again.

"Him flashing lights all hours of the night and they got them newfangled drones flying around buzzing my cattle. It's not right I tell you. It's not right." I took a sip of my tea and let her continue on. "Saturday night, he was shining lights right in my window, I could hear the cows complainin' somewhat fierce."

"Wow, that is pretty rude," I commented wanting to give that guy a piece of my mind myself.

"Next day they wasn't wantin' to eat. It's not right," she grumbled again. "I complained to the sheriff but they won't do anything, but give them a warning. It's just a waste of time. I've a good mind to move."

"I'm so sorry to hear that, Betty. It's got to be hard taking care of all this property. Do you have anyone to help you?"

"Well, Jerry next door, he sometimes comes and helps, especially in the winter time. He's a good guy, that Jerry is." Betty leaned over the table to me. "Between you and me, he could do better, that wife of his is loony," and she spun her hand around her ear when she said it.

I couldn't help but laugh. "Sorry, but I think you're right. Don't tell her I said that, she's my client."

"You know I won't. I saw the police over there, care to share?" she lifted her eyebrows at me over the rim of her cup.

"Are you the one who reported the bones in your yard?"

"Yes, ma'am. I've got a reputation to uphold after all," she said and winked at me. "Normally, I wouldn't, Carol and I get along pretty well, but I told her that her pipes were too close to the surface and not to drive over them or they'd break. The previous owner was a lazy summabitch and only put them six inches under the ground. He didn't listen to me either. Now I've got my pipes buried a good foot in the ground, which is a good thing because Carol had to have the truck towed the other day after it got stuck in the mud from her broken pipe. How embarrassing having your truck towed from your backyard. People gotta think," she said, tapping her index finger on her temple.

"Yes, they do," I agreed. Are you the neighbor that called the police on Carol?"

Betty looked a little sheepish. "I'm afraid I did. She didn't fix the pipe right away and that water leaked all day, washing those bones onto my property. And besides. I got a reputation to uphold."

"Being cranky?"

"Exactly," she replied, taking a sip of tea and looking at me over the rim.

"You seem like a nice young woman, Holly. Let me give you a bit of advice, stay away from Bonnie, she's no good and she'll get you in trouble." Betty suddenly stood up. "I've taken up enough of your time. Sorry, I was so disagreeable but I hate those door sales people. If you don't mind, when you go by Mike's place, please ask him to tone it down with the lights. He'll take it a lot easier coming from a pretty girl like yourself."

A bit taken aback by the stream of words, I thanked her again for the tea and promised to do just that. Mentally, I adjusted my impression of her from grumpy old neighbor to sweet old lady. Sometimes first impressions are wrong I guess.

MIKE

I tromped next door to Mike's because there are no sidewalks out here in the country and it's pretty weedy by the road. Yes, I used the cranky store lady's word because it really seemed to fit. I won't lie, the extra weight I carried wasn't doing me any good either and maybe this exercise would help me shed a few pounds.

Mike's house was a single story that had clearly seen better days. While Betty's was a little worn, this one was downright falling apart. The roof was missing a few shingles and the outside paint was peeling. Heck the lawn was more dirt and weeds than grass.

The one aberration was a classic 1968 Pontiac Lemans GTO convertible in pristine condition parked in the open garage which had apparently recently been washed and polished. Hey, just because I'm a girl doesn't mean I can't appreciate a good classic car. I felt like I had seen it before but couldn't place it. Well, I couldn't place it at this moment. Give my brain five minutes and it would just pop in out of the blue. That's just the way brains work as you get older.

Proceeding past the car I stepped over a watering hose that was leaking but caked with dried mud and past a wall sconce with wires hanging to the ground. What is with these people? Isn't anyone worried about water bills? Typical car fiend. Keep the car immaculate and let everything else go. I knocked lightly on the door, mainly because I didn't want any splinters in my knuckles.

A good looking muscley guy in his late forties with messy blonde hair answered the door. "Hey," he said.

Okay, that's different. "Hey," I answered back. "Are you Mike? Betty next door told me your name."

"Yeah, she's a real peach," he answered sarcastically.

"Well, I'm Holly from Front Door Realty, I'm selling Carol's place down the street. Can I talk to you for a few minutes?"

"Yeah, sure, what's up?"

"Well, like I said, I'm selling Carol's house. The market is up right now and I'm just wondering if you'd be interested in knowing the current value of your home? Oh, I noticed the wires on your light there, you know solar will save you money and increase the value of your home as well."

"I would care if I owned it, but I'm renting, sooo," he lifted his shoulders in a shrug. "About the only thing I really do own is that car in the garage and I'm selling it. It runs great. I'd start it for you but it's missing a battery."

"Nice, car. 1968 right?" I asked.

"Wow, I'm impressed, you know your cars," he stated with a little more emphasis on "impressed" than was really necessary. I instantly pegged him as one of those chauvinistic types who like to placate women.

"I do indeed know my cars, Mike. Oh, I do need to pass on a message from Betty next door. She would appreciate it if you wouldn't continue to shine lights in her back yard. I guess it bothers the cows." I added pointedly before he felt it necessary to dispel any knowledge I possessed about cars.

"Lights?" for a moment he seemed puzzled. "When did she see the lights?"

I shrugged my shoulders. "I don't know. Maybe over the weekend?"

"Lights, lights...Oh," his eyes lit up. "Must've been Saturday night. I had the local robotics team over to practice flying drones."

"In the rain?" I questioned.

"It didn't start raining until later. I used to work in the movie business as a stunt man. I was teaching the kids how to do a light show with drones. It's really cool actually," he began. Fearing he was going to go on a long unnecessary explanation I cut him off.

"That is really cool. Well, if you ever want to buy a house, give me a call," I said, handing him my business card. "I work with lenders too in case you need any help with that as well." A shadow crossed his face so fast, I wondered if I had seen it. Something had changed in his attitude though and I made my goodbyes and scurried back to my car pausing by the light with the wires.

"You know, you really should fix this, someone could get hurt."

"Thanks for pointing that out," he said snippily, "I'll get right on that."

At this point I'm wondering why I'm even door knocking but you've got to play the percentages. The next house was around the corner and up the hill a bit. Definitely getting my exercise today. This house was really cute in shades of green with gingerbread trim. Knocking on the door brought the sound of a small dog yapping but no one answered. I knocked again to be sure but when no one came to the door, I walked next door.

his house was a tri-level log house built up against the hillside. The door was answered at my first knock by none other than Jacob. Mentally screaming in my head at my misfortune, I politely said, "Hello Jacob. I'm just in the neighborhood door knocking. You have such a beautiful house here. I'm wondering why you would want to buy Carol's house? Your's is clearly the nicer house."

"It really isn't any of your business now is it? Is Carol ready to sell to me?" he snapped.

I failed to withhold an audible sigh. "No, I've explained to you...."

"Well just let me know when she is. Once they find Jerry's dead, she'll be ready to sell." He then shut the door in my face.

"Wow." The word left my mouth involuntarily. Now thoroughly depressed, I walked back to my car with my head low. Time to cut my losses and have a go another day.

CANCELLATIONS

Ready to head back into town, I put in a call from my car to the Hotchkiss's to make sure we were still on for our listing appointment. Things come up you know?

"Hotchkiss residence."

"Hi, this is Holly Holcraft. I'm just calling to confirm our appointment for tonight at 6," I stated in a cheery voice.

"Your appointment? I'm sorry, I don't understand. Your assistant rescheduled for this morning and then you didn't show."

My heart dropped into my feet. "Is this Mrs. Hotchkiss? I didn't reschedule," I answered wondering why Joe would have done such a thing without telling me.

"I'm sorry, but she definitely said she was your assistant and when you didn't show we decided to go with someone else. Again I'm terribly sorry," and then the line went dead.

Shock coursed through my body and I couldn't think. Just no, no, no, this wasn't happening. I worked so hard for this. Wait, did she say, "she?" My assistant is not a she. Who would have called? Who even knew I had the appointment besides Joe? It took a moment for realization to hit, but then I had a good idea who it could be. Bonnie. Definitely a 'she' and definitely dislikes me. Wow. I knew she was vindictive but this really was a new low.

I drove slowly home, my mind in a whirl. It had never been guaranteed that I would get the Hotchkiss listing but this just pulled the rug out from under my feet. At least before I had a chance. Now I had nothing. Sure, I have other transactions. The Makimotos will be going under contract soon. I crossed my fingers. The Marples will be closing soon, I hope, but Bonnie is the other agent and she seems to drag out all my transactions with her. Mark Brown's smelly house offer should be accepted and closed in the next ten days. Nobody but an investor is going to buy that house. I blew my lips out. The Hotchkiss listing would get me out of debt, the rest just kept me surviving. I'm getting tired of just surviving.

Pulling into my drive, I could see Ginger in the front window, waiting for me, her little tail wagging like a propeller. Even her cute face could barely cheer me right now but it was good to know someone was happy to see me.

After I fed Ginger, I grabbed a glass of wine and plopped in front of the television. Maybe I could distract myself with someone else's problems even if they were imaginary.

My evening of self commiseration was interrupted by the chime of the phone.

"Hello Vana."

"What happened?" she immediately questioned. She knew me so well.

"I've had a horrible day," I answered, beginning to cry. "That horrible Bonnie Belmar is what happened," I gasped out between sobs. "She sabotaged my appointment with the Hotchkisses and stole my listing."

"Are you sure?"

"They said they went with someone else. Mrs. Hotchkiss said my assistant rescheduled my appointment and she referred to them as a "she." Who else would it be?"

"Oh, Hol, I'm so sorry. I don't know why she has to be such a witch to you." commiserated Vana. "I don't have any problems with her, well, except for her silent condemnation of our friendship. I probably shouldn't have mentioned that. Hey, I know, why don't we take off tomorrow evening and go do something. They have an escape room in Morecroft that I've been wanting to try."

"An escape room? What is that?"

"You get locked in a room filled with puzzles and clues and you have to figure them out to escape," she explained excitedly. In fact, I don't think I had ever heardher so excited.

"Yeah, I'm not so..." I paused. What would it hurt. "Okay, fine but how about Saturday night?" I suggested hopefully.

"Oh no, no, no. You have a date Saturday night and you're not getting out of it."

"Well, he could come with us. It could be a double date," I suggested, again hopefully.

The silence on the phone showed she saw through my plan. "Fine. But I get to choose the room."

"Fine. It's a date. On Saturday. With you and Bob and ?

"Lamar."

"Really? You couldn't find a Dave or Ken?"

"Come on, you know those are a dime a dozen. Lamar is unique."

"Don't tell me he has a great personality."

"Okay, I won't."

TRAVIS

It's Thursday and my life sucks right now. I have bills I can't pay. I lost the Hotchkiss listing. Through no fault of my own, I might add. Emmeline is never going to pick a house and Bonnie represents the seller for the Makimoto's deal AND the buyer on the Marple's house. Maybe I'll just stay in bed all day. I put my pillow over my head and screamed into it.

Pausing for air, I thought of Carol. I'm probably going to lose Carol's listing due to Jerry's death, if he is dead. I really need to find that out. Speaking of Carol, I was so busy yesterday I completely forgot to check in with her. Maybe she has an update.

I was about to call her when my phone buzzed, it was Joe. Composing myself I answered, "Hello Joe, good news I hope?"

"Well, sort of. Bonnie scheduled the home inspection for Friday."

"Well of course she would do it the very last day possible. Thanks for the update Joe. I was just about to call Carol and check in with her. Have you heard anything?"

"No, nothing."

"I guess no news is good news. Oh, Joe? Who told you that Jerry was dead?" There was a moment of silence from the other end of the line. "Joe, you there?"

"Yeah, it was a friend of mine who works in the tech department. Why do you ask?"

"Well, the police haven't told Carol yet, and I was just wondering why."

"Huh, well that is weird. I've got to run, I'll talk to you later," and then he was gone.

I called Carol from my bed. She answered on the first ring.

"Hi hun, it's Holly. I just called to check and see how you are doing."

"It's just terrible Holly. I haven't heard a word from the police and I can't reach Jerry. I'm really worried about him. What if something really terrible happened to him? I know we're getting divorced but I do still love him."

"I know you do honey. So the police never actually said he was dead?"

"No. He's missing. Well, I mean, they can't find him," she stated emphatically.

Well that was interesting. Why did Joe say he was dead if the police thought he was just missing? But Penny said there was a body in his apartment. Maybe I should try to get a hold of her again but I wouldn't want to risk getting her in trouble. No. I needed to find out some other way and not from that horrible detective Moran.

Making a decision, I swung my legs over the side of the bed to sit up. "Carol, honey, I am so sorry about all this and I promise to help however I can. You just hang in there okay? If the police haven't said he's dead then we're going to believe that he's not."

Carol sniffed, "Thank you Holly. I will keep trying to reach him. And thank you for all your help." I ended the call and placed another.

"Morecroft Police Department," answered a female voice.

"Hi, my name is Holly, can you tell me who is handling the Oates investigation?"

"Just a minute." I heard paper rustling and then a moment later, "Detective Smart can speak with you"

"That would be great," I replied. A moment later a new voice came on the line.

"Detective Travis Smart, do you have information on the Oates case?"

"Hello, detective, my name is Holly and I'm the real estate agent for Carol Oates. I just wanted to confirm that Jerry is dead because it will affect the transaction."

"Why do you think Mr. Oates is dead?" he replied, sounding puzzled.

Thrown off for a second it took me a bit to respond. "Isn't he? My assistant said someone in the department told him they found his body in his apartment."

"Mmhmm. No, he's not dead, not that we know of any way but we haven't been able to reach him. Do you know where he is?"

"Mr. Oates? Carol said he went camping. In fact, he's expected back to sign papers. Why does Carol think that you think that she killed him?"

"I think you're confused," he replied. "As far as we know Jerry is just missing."

"But there were bones?" I asked.

"Just animal bones," he replied.

"So no one's dead."

There was a long silence then, "Since it'll probably be on the news soon, I'll tell you. A person was found dead in Jerry's apartment. That's why we're looking for him. It looks like a random home invasion, we just need to clarify who he was. Would you give me a call if you hear from him?"

"Um, sure, I suppose I could do that. So, Carol's not under suspicion?"

"Not if Jerry shows up."

This conversation just left me with more questions than answers. Who was the dead guy? Did Jerry kill him? But no, the police didn't say he was under suspicion. Why would Joe's friend tell him it was Jerry if the police knew it wasn't. If Carol didn't kill Jerry, where did the finger bone come from and whose was it?

Checking my missed calls, I discovered the home inspection for Carol's house was back on for 10 a.m. this morning. Ugh, she could have at least mentioned that. To my chagrin I discovered it was nearly 9 a.m. I rushed through dressing and left the house with no coffee and no breakfast.

I pulled up to Carol's house with two minutes to spare. The inspector pulled up behind me in a white truck. Glancing in the mirror, I fixed my hair and plastered a smile I didn't feel on my face. If Carol didn't have that garage cleaned I was going to kill her myself.

"Hello Tom," I said, extending my hand to the kindly old man. "Thank you so much for rescheduling."

Tom laughed. "You've given me plenty of business, I figured I owed you one," he replied, taking my hand. Shaking his head he added, "This was a first for me. Can't quite see why she would do that but..." his voice trailed off in bewilderment. Tom Handy had been an inspector for 25 years, now in his early sixties, for him to say this was a first was really saying something.

But what could he say? What could anyone say? There was no explanation for feeding a pig to your dogs in the garage. Unless you were covering up a crime?

Tom's voice startled me from my thoughts. "Well, let's go on in and take a look."

"Yes, let's," I replied with my fingers crossed. Thankfully, all evidence, and smell, of the pig was gone. My phone rang in my pocket but I silenced it without looking. The priority here was to get the inspection done.

Carol was waiting for us and looking as if she hadn't slept for the past three days.

"Carol I just wanted to say again how sorry I am that I haven't talked to you."

"It's okay. Don't worry about it. I know how busy you are. I'm just glad that you're even helping me. I'm really, really sorry about the whole pig thing. I don't know what I was thinking."

Probably not thinking but instead I said, "not to worry. Tom's here to reinspect and then everything should go smoothly. The buyer's loan is approved. We just need this done," I said crossing my fingers behind my back. And for Jerry to show up and sign the papers but I wasn't going to mention that in front of Carol. She looked as if she was ready to cry.

Now that the floor was cleaned it clearly showed a white splotch. "Carol, what's the white stain? I don't remember seeing that before."

"Oh, oh that. That's just some acid, I was making a gift for my niece and it must have spilled."

"Acid?"

"Yeah, you know for etching glass."

"Well, it looks really bad. Tom, is there any way to fix that?" I asked.

Tom knelt down and scratched at it with a fingernail. "'Fraid not," he replied. "Once it's eaten into the concrete like that, you'd have to paint over it to cover it. It's harmless though."

Looking around I noticed a missing item, memories of that television show 'Breaking Bad' went through my mind.

"Oh my God."

"What?" questioned Carol and Tom together. Oops did I say that out loud?

"What happened to that antique tub you had in here?" I asked her.

"The tub?" she asked, puzzled. I could see in her eyes as she made the connection. "Are you accusing me of killing my husband?" she cried in disbelief. "I saw that show too and I can't believe you."

"Well you have to admit, it does look suspicious. There was a tub here and now there's not but there's an acid stain on the floor."

"I gave that tub to my neighbor for her cows. She wanted to use it for a watering trough. You can ask Mike, he took it over," she declared outraged.

"When did he deliver the tub? It was here on Tuesday."

"Why, he didn't pick it up until Wednesday. He was supposed to get it on Saturday night but never showed."

"How did he move it? I didn't see a truck at his house?"

"He used mine to take it to Betty's. It's just next door."

"I thought no one liked Betty?"

"I dunno, he does things for her."

"She said Jerry helps her out?"

"Just the animals. Mike sometimes does things around the house for her."

"You guys sure do a lot for someone you don't like very much."

"Neighbors. We gotta stick together."

Sudden inspiration struck me. "Do you know her sister Bonnie?"

"Oh, Betty doesn't talk about her," Carol said shaking her head sadly. "She showed up once and Betty refused to answer the door."

I was going to say I was sorry, but my head had other ideas. "Carol, why do the police think you killed your husband?"

"I told you because of the bones in the yard," she wailed. "I thought you were my friend."

"I'm sorry Carol, I am your friend, but I had to ask. You're my client and I need to know the truth so I can help you. I don't believe you would kill your husband."

"I don't either," put in Tom, startling both of us because we had forgotten he was there. "I think I can honestly say, this isn't the type of acid you would use to dissolve a body anyway, plus it would totally ruin the finish on the tub."

"Well that's good to know." Turning to Carol I asked, "You said you gave it to Betty?"

"I thought you said you believed me!"

"I do, but if I can get a picture of the tub, that will prove to the police that you didn't have anything to do with it. That's the only reason I asked," I lied.

"Oh, well yes I gave it to Betty, next door. Is, is the inspection okay?" she added hesitantly.

Tom laughed, "Yes, the home inspection is fine, there's no major problems. I think we're good. Just be glad about one thing."

"What's that?"

"The buyer's weren't here."

UNEXPECTED SURPRISES

After leaving Carol's I figured I could get one issue out of the way so I cut across the yard to get to Betty's.

Betty answered my knock with a glare on her face. "Oh, it's you," she said, relaxing the glare but still blocking the door.

"Hi Betty. I'm really sorry to bother you but I'm just trying to help Carol out and I had a few questions if you don't mind."

"Fire away, it's never stopped you before."

"Mm okay. Um Carol said she gave you her claw foot bathtub for your animals?"

"Yeah she gave me the tub, Mike brought it over." Betty was nothing if not succinct.

"Would you mind if I took a picture of it?" I smiled apologetically. "I'm just trying to clear Carol's name."

"Hmpfh." Betty crossed her arms and looked down her nose at me, which honestly, isn't difficult as I'm shorter than most people."

"Did I do something to offend you?"

Betty let out a huge sigh. "Why do you ask so many questions anyway? You were askin' bout the tub. Well I got it for my animals.

Danged thing had the paint peeling off. Thought it would make my cows sick so I turned it into a planter instead. You should have seen it when you come up the drive," she said.

I turned to look back down the drive. Yup there it was at the end of the drive planted with pansies. So much for a picture of the inside. I turned back around.

"Guess I wasn't paying attention." Her suspicious gaze told me she knew very well I had not.

Betty looked left and right then grabbed my arm and pulled me in the house, shutting the door behind us.

"You don't rile easily do you?" She asked me dropping my arm.

"Are you trying to rile me? Correct me if I'm wrong, but I thought we were on better terms the last time we met."

Betty smiled which suddenly transformed her whole face. "I got a reputation to uphold. Once you let people know you're friendly, the next thing you know they want to come over and visit."

"Would that be so bad?"

"Not really, but I prefer the solitude. It helps keep me on track while I write."

"You're a writer? What kinds of things do you write?"

"Promise you won't tell?"

"Of course."

"You know the author Ophelia Love?"

"The erotic author?" My mouth dropped open in shock.

"Yup, that's me," she proclaimed proudly. "What else is an old lady supposed to do in a house by herself?"

"Oh my," I giggled behind my hand. "Wow, that's pretty amazing. Good for you and nice touch with the name. Don't worry, I'll keep your reputation intact."

As I turned to leave, Betty grabbed my arm. "Holly, how did your husband die?"

"How did you know he died?"

"A woman can tell."

"It was a car accident. Drunk driver forced him off the road."

"I'm really sorry to hear that. It must have been hard to carry on without him with a small child."

"Yes, yes it was." Although it had been ten years, sadness threatened to overwhelm me. Curse those menopause emotions. "I've got to go. I'll talk to you later." Betty just nodded as I opened the door. As it closed behind me, I yelled through it, "Sorry I bothered you. It won't happen again." Then I walked grumpily to my car and slammed the door shut when I got in. That should keep her reputation intact.

Headed back to the office, I stopped in at Katie May's to grab a bite for lunch. I was feeling a little glum and my timing was definitely off today as nearly every table was filled which didn't help to improve my mood.

"There's an empty table in the back," yelled Katie to me as she indicated towards the back left of the restaurant.

Shuffling through the patrons, I found the empty table and sat down. Katie showed up right behind me with a diet coke, she knows me so well, and I placed my order. Nothing special, just a turkey sandwich with a side salad, ranch dressing. I began thumbing through my email on my phone when I was interrupted by a cranky voice above the din in the restaurant.

"You need to move."

"What?"

"You're just drinking a soda and I need a place to eat my lunch, so you need to move."

My stubborn mom mood instantly kicked in at the tone in her voice. "That's nice," I replied as I continued scrolling through my phone. The woman stood there out of my line of sight hrmpfhing. I refuse to indulge rude people.

"You're welcome to sit at my table but I'm not moving," I finally said without looking up. The chair scraped across the ground as she pulled it out and settled her food on the table. A very nice young man walked up with my food and set it in front of me. Shock crossed my face as I looked up.

"It's you!" I said, narrowing my eyes at her.

"You didn't say you were eating," she retorted sharply as if that made a difference.

"You didn't ask."

"I wouldn't have bothered you if you were eating," she mumbled into her food.

"Are you sure about that? You're the woman who was commenting on how fat I was in the check out line."

"I only said you didn't need that donut. I won't apologize for the truth," she stated matter of factly, looking up at me and swishing her blonde hair back.

"So you do remember me. What's your name?"

"Maggie," she said reluctantly.

"It must be exhausting for you."

"What's that?"

"Being angry. It's got to be hard to be angry all the time."

"What makes you think I'm angry?" She snapped.

"Um, that." I paused to really look at her. Dark circles under her eyes and brown lines spoke to stress. If there's one thing another woman understands, it's stress. "Is there anything I can help you with?"

"Why would you do that? You don't even know me," she asked suspiciously.

"Look," I said, deciding to restart the entire conversation. "Let's begin again shall we? It's very nice to meet you Maggie. My name is Holly, I'm a real estate agent and I enjoy powdered sugar donuts on stressful days."

There was a very long silence before Maggie spoke again.

"Nice to meet you Holly," she said grudgingly. "My kids do say I'm perhaps too judgmental. Thank you for letting me sit here."

"You're welcome." We both continued to eat in silence. What did I really expect? People who are grouchy and judgmental are not likely to change over a greeting but the silence was welcome. Maggie didn't look like your typical 'Karen,' rather she seemed like a woman who maybe had a hard life. You never know what someone is going through although there are people who are just not nice, like Bonnie. Hmmm, that gave me a moment's pause. What happened to Bonnie to make her so mean? She didn't have a problem with Vana. I would have to look into that.

"Perhaps I was a little harsh in the store but a pretty woman like you should be mindful of her weight. It was just concern."

I took a sip of soda contemplating her sort of apology then looked at Maggie.

"Can I ask you a question?"

"I can't stop you."

"Why do you get your food to go if you're going to eat here?"

Maggie took another bite before answering. "If you eat here they charge tax, but if you take it to go, they don't."

Well I guess that made sense. "It was nice meeting you again and having lunch together," I said as I stood and gathered my things. "Maybe we'll run into each other again."

As I walked away she yelled after me, "we're not friends," which just made me giggle to myself.

JOE

Joe was in the office when I got there. He had only worked for me for a few months but I already felt he was indispensable. He was focused on his computer, getting work done as usual. The office was a little tight with two people working in it but I liked to think of it as cozy. Besides Joe was pretty tiny as guys go, not that I would ever comment on that to him. He was nearly as short as me and slim with sandy blond hair and brown eyes. He wasn't really spectacular in any sort of way but his enthusiasm was catching and he always seemed to have a smirk on his face as if he knew something no one else did.

"Any updates on the files?" I asked.

"Not really. The Marples home inspection is tomorrow," he answered, "and I've received all the paperwork on the Oates file..." his voice trailed off.

"Thanks Joe." I smiled. "Hopefully, we'll get these all closed." Positive thinking, that's the ticket.

I sat down at my own computer and started sorting through my thousands of emails. Okay, I'm exaggerating. Yes, I do have over 5,000 emails in my inbox but really only a few dozen came in today. Someday I am going to clean them out, just, not today.

"Yes!" I exclaimed loudly. Joe jumped in his chair. "Oh sorry, Joe. Mark Brown's offer on the smelly house has been accepted. Um, you wouldn't want to do the inspection on that one would you?"

As Joe opened his mouth to politely decline, I jumped in first. "I'm just kidding. He's not doing one. He basically did it on Tuesday. But you should have seen your face," I said as we laughed together. It felt good to laugh with a friend.

Fishing my phone from my purse, I punched in the numbers for the Makimotos.

"Hello Holly." Toni Makimoto's musical voice answered the phone. "How are you?"

"I'm great, Toni. I'm just calling to see if you wanted to look at any more homes?"

"I think we're done looking at houses," she answered making my heart plunge to my stomach. "We've decided to put in an offer on the Tudor."

"You have?" I asked elated.

"Yes, as long as the house is cleaned before closing and after Mr. Hajari moves out," yelled Mori in the background.Toni giggled.

I smiled and shook my head. It was like dealing with children. "Of course. I will send over the paperwork for you to sign electronically and I look forward to working with you on this deal."

"Thank you Holly. My husband just loves that house, especially the kitchen. I'll keep an eye out for your email."

I leaned back in my chair and raised my fist to the ceiling. "Yes!"

Joe was looking at me expectantly as I ended the call with a huge smile on my face. "That was Toni Makimoto. They are going to make an offer on the Tudor. I knew they would love that kitchen."

"That's awesome. Um, not to change the mood but isn't that Bonnie's?"

I sighed. It was always a sigh when Bonnie was involved and having her on the other side of two of my transactions was enough to make me grind my teeth. I don't like to think ill of people but there was just something so rotten about her.

"Yes, yes it is but she can't screw around with every deal. She needs to make money too. Right?"

I noticed Joe made no comment but he was usually like that, trying to keep the peace. He was a great assistant.

"So currently we have:

Makimoto's offer to present.

Marples are scheduled to close next Friday. Fingers crossed.

Mark Brown's offer has been accepted. And that just leaves Emmeline who still hasn't picked a house."

"And probably never will. What happened with the Hotchkiss listing?" he asked the dreaded question.

"Nothing, that's what happened. I think Bonnie pretended to be my assistant and cheated me out of it."

Disbelief filled his face. "No way! What are you going to do?"

"What can I do? I have no proof. I'm just going to focus on what I can do."

"What about the Oates? Do you have to cancel?"

"Well here's the funny thing about that," I began when we were interrupted by a knock at the door which turned out to be a tall handsome stranger. Six foot two, with eyes of blue. Was that a cliche?

"Hi," said the gorgeous man. "Are you Holly?" I couldn't answer right away because I was wondering if I should pinch myself. Gorgeous guys just don't come knocking on my door. Especially in Appleby.

Joe gave the man a look and then said, "If you don't mind, I'm going to go take lunch," and left. I barely noticed because I was entranced by the stranger's blue eyes which looked puzzled prompting me to realize I hadn't answered his question.

"Um, Yes, I'm Holly and you are?"

"I'm Detective Smart from Morecroft. We talked on the phone. I wanted to introduce myself and ask you some questions."

"Me? I don't know that I can help you," I began.

"Carol said you'd lived here all your life and know most of the people."

"Well, I am in real estate," I said with a bit of pride. "Next to grocery clerks, we probably see most everyone," I added nonchalantly.

His phone buzzed and he glanced at the screen, then sighed, before speaking. "Looks like I've got to go see some other people right now, can we meet up later?" he asked.

Disappointment welled in my heart. "Yeah, sure. Tell me where and when." You bet your sweet tushy we can. Oh my gosh, I sound like Lucy.

Handing me his card, he said, "Great. I'll call you when I'm done, is that okay?"

"Sounds great," I answered, handing him my card. "I'll see you later then." The door closed behind him but my eyes were still locked on the door he went through. When my phone beeped. What is wrong with me? I felt feelings I hadn't had in ten years.

After he left I read his card, Detective Travis Smart. Well he certainly looked smart to me. And handsome. My phone beeped to remind me I had a missed call. I had to add that notification to my phone because I kept forgetting to check it when I was busy. My heart jumped, it was from Mrs. Hotchkiss.

A SECOND CHANCE

"Hi Holly. This is Alma Hotchkiss." Her voice came clearly through the line. "I ran into Betty and she mentioned that you were helping her neighbor Carol to get out of trouble. I've decided to give you a second chance because I like how you go above and beyond for your clients. Don't mess this up. I'll see you this afternoon at 5 p.m."

Oh awesome! I was suddenly so excited. Wow a handsome stranger and a second chance, today really was turning around. Today at 5. Shoot today at 5! It was 3:30 already. I frantically hunted through my stuff for my listing presentation. Found it! Oh, I was really not dressed for an interview because I had gone to the home inspection at Carol's this morning. Heels and weeds just don't mix well. Unfortunately, I didn't have time to change, so I grabbed my stuff and headed for the car.

Just so you know, our office is located in this cute mall with a pretty green lawn edging it. It's just a little strip that you can't do anything with but dogs seem to like it, which was really unfortunate because one currently had some business to conduct and I don't mean real estate business. At 5 feet 2 inches tall, I prefer to wear wedges to elevate my height a little just so I don't always have to look up at people. Plus they're flat on the bottom. Fishing in my purse for my keys I neglected to see said dog.

I think you can see where this is going. I saw the dog pooping in time to avoid the hot mess but stepping over it left my foot half on the hard concrete and half on the wet soggy grass. With a sinking feeling I realized I was going down. I tried to stop my momentum but the soggy lawn sucked onto my shoe and wasn't letting go without a fight. Fortunately, I missed the dog poop, unfortunately, I didn't miss landing on the wet lawn. "Stupid dog," I yelled at it angrily from the ground. The dog scuffed at the lawn with it's hind feet, gave a little "tut tut" with its nose in the air and slowly sauntered off. Argh, I had no time for this.

Struggling to my feet, my butt was now covered in mud. There was nothing for it, but I was going to have to go home and change. Why did there have to be so many ups and downs in ONE DAY!

I threw all my stuff in my car and turned the key. Nothing. "Are you kidding me right now!" I yelled. Remembering what Amos had said, poor man, I pulled the hood release, I opened it and wiggled the battery cable. Jumping back in my seat I tried the key again and the car roared to life. As I peeled out of the parking lot I saw Omar walking towards my car with a surprised look on his face.

At 7:30 that evening I met the detective at Tipsy's, the local fine dining establishment. My stomach was all twisted in knots. Whether it was because he was so handsome or I was afraid of what he had to say about the Oates', I didn't know. Both thoughts distressed me.

Detective Travis Smart was not only handsome, he was also intelligent and single. Not that I was looking mind you, but it was a nice detail.

"Wow, you look really nice," he commented. "I mean not that you didn't before, it's just you didn't have to get dressed up for me."

"Don't flatter yourself." I laughed. "I had an interview earlier and had to change. Detective Smart I'm a little confused. If Jerry's alive, what questions do you have?"

"Well," he said and then was quiet as the waitress came to take our drink order. We had settled ourselves in a booth in the corner of the restaurant which was pretty much devoid of patrons on a Thursday night. This place was higher on the scale than Katie Mays and was filled with deep wine colored booths, the space in the center of the restaurant filled with tables covered with white table cloths and flowers. The window here gave a view onto the lake and he gazed out them for a moment..

"I understand you had a dead battery on Tuesday morning."

"Yes," I said surprised. "How did you know?"

"I was going through Amos Belroy's logs and you were his last call."

"The tow truck driver? I don't understand. I thought you were looking for Jerry Oates."

"No, I'm here to find out what happened to Amos."

"I thought he died from a heart attack."

"He did, but the coroner found a head wound that shouldn't be there."

"Are you saying he was murdered?" I whispered, my eyes wide.

Travis looked around before continuing, "I don't know but it doesn't make sense. I know Amos and he was meticulous about his truck. No way would he have a brake line in such bad condition it would fail."

"I'm sorry, he seemed like a really nice guy."

"He was. Did he say anything to you about where his next call was?"

"No, I'm sorry, we just talked about batteries and then he left."

The waitress interrupted us to take our food order and deliver our drinks and then left.

"If you don't mind," I asked. "What happened at Jerry's apartment?" I fiddled with the silverware nervously.

"Looks like a home invasion and the victim was hit over the back of the head. We've got no clues, there were no cameras. Honestly, it probably won't get solved."

"Wow, that's too bad."

Our food came and we ate in silence for a while. "I meant to ask you," said the detective looking at me with his gorgeous blue eyes, "Who told your assistant Jerry was the victim? I don't want to get anyone in trouble, but if there's a leak in the department I need to know."

I tried to think back on our conversation. "Joe said it was a friend, he said 'she,' I don't think he ever gave a name. You know I thought the whole thing was weird because the police never told Carol her husband was dead."

"They wouldn't do that. If he was dead they would have notified or arrested her," he said. "I mean they wouldn't let her think he was alive if he was dead." He took a bite of food. "I checked the techs who worked the scene. They were all people I know and none of them were female which makes me wonder where Joe really got his information from. I think I need to have a talk with him."

"You don't think he had anything to do with it?" I questioned.

"I don't know what to think," he replied seriously. "Did he know where Jerry lived?"

Did he know? Did I give him Jerry's address? Did I have Jerry's address? I had given his contact information to escrow and they had sent the paperwork to him. My brain hurt trying to remember. I realized Travis was waiting on a response.

"No. Yes. I mean he could have, he's my assistant and he has to send paperwork sometimes, but it's usually electronically." I shook my head. "No, Joe's great. He's like my right hand, I can't believe he would have anything to do with this."

Travis shook his handsome head slowly, "People get fooled all the time. I'll have to check into it all the same. Please don't say anything to him."

"I won't but I know you're wrong," I replied. Travis sipped his tea then relaxed back into his seat.

"You said you went to an interview. How did it go? If you don't mind my asking."

"I was late. It didn't happen and it was my second chance."

"You seem pretty cheery about that,"

"I listened to the message late, my car wouldn't start, I ruined my pants when I fell in the muddy lawn. It just wasn't meant to be." We both had a laugh as I filled him in on the dog hijinks. The skin by his blue eyes crinkled when he laughed just as Evan's had. The thought of my husband made me feel guilty.

"Sorry to hear all that. Wait, your car wouldn't start? With a new battery?

"I thought it was weird too but it was just a loose cable."

"Oh," he glanced at his plate thoughtfully.

"What?"

"Nothing, it's just I can't imagine Amos would leave a battery cable loose.

"Do you find conspiracies everywhere?"

"When you've seen what I've seen I find it's good to be cautious," Travis swirled the ice in his glass before taking a sip.

"Probably right about that," I said as Omar's face watching me leave the office popped into my head.

Looking around the restaurant, I spotted Bonnie in a booth glaring at me, her lip twitching as if she was muttering to herself. She turned her head immediately feigning interest but I knew what I saw.

"Would you excuse me for a minute?" pushing back my chair and putting on a dazzling smile I walked over to her.

"Oh Bonnie, I'm so glad to run into you. I need to talk to you about the Marple house..."

Bonnie cut in rudely. "There's nothing to talk about. It's going to take as long as it takes. They are difficult to deal with and I can't make them do anything. I can't help it if you don't understand."

Holly smiled sweetly. "Oh, I understand and I'm so incredibly busy right now so I've transferred the listing to Vana."

"You did what?" she sputtered.

"Transferred the listing to Vana. I hope you don't mind. She had a little spare time and was more than willing to take it. I was just having lunch with Travis when I spotted you," I turned to wave at him, mainly to hide the smile starting at Bonnie's obvious distress. "He's a detective in Morecroft. Her eyes widened at the news. Well I'll leave you to your lunch. Have a good night."

The startled look on her face was very satisfying as I returned to our table. After saying good bye to Travis and getting in my car, I put in a quick call to Vana. "Hey, Vi, I uh, I told Bonnie I transferred my Marple listing to you. I hope you don't mind."

"I don't mind but why would you do that?" she questioned.

I laughed. "I just ran into her at Tipsy's and she was staring daggers at me during dinner and I just, I don't know what came over me. She was just making me so angry and frustrated and I know you two get along so..." my voice tapered off as I ran out of words to say. I didn't in fact know why I had done it. I just wanted the escrow to close and to get her goat.

Vana's voice came back over the line. "Eating dinner at Tipsy's huh? Not your usual choice."

Uh oh. I can't hide anything from Vana. Or lie to her. "If you must know," I began with mock indignation when a beep interrupted us.

"Oh, oh that's Bonnie beeping in now. Must want to confirm with me. I'll call you later and you can fill me in on your 'date.'"

"It wasn't a da..." but she was already gone.

INSOMNIA

It's 1 am and I can't sleep. Snuggled in bed with Ginger, my mind keeps running in circles. My life is usually busy with clients and family but not like this. There's so much drama and mystery right now. Give me a difficult transaction any day and I can fix it but this? I don't know anything about murders or criminals. The good news was that Carol wasn't under suspicion and Jerry's not dead, so there's that. But what happened to poor sweet Amos?

Normally my home is my retreat. It was a fixer upper and it was remodeled with relaxation in mind. Cool blues with white furniture in the bedroom, a lovely cream throughout the halls and living room; natural wood furniture; comfy plush area rugs; and a bright, sunny, dream kitchen which I rarely cooked in because it was just me now. I really enjoy it when I make coffee in the morning and the wine glasses in the under cabinet rack sparkle in the sunlight. You really need to enjoy the small things.

The hours crept by and realization that I had fallen asleep came when the morning sun hit my eyes. Ginger had taken the opportunity to snuggle against my back. Her warm weight was a pleasant feeling this morning. My phone buzzing dashed the moment away.

I answered only to hold the phone away from my head as Bonnie's incessant screeching filled the air.

"How dare you accuse me of stealing your listing, you irritating little twit. You have no right meddling in people's lives! I'll have your license for this!"

I could picture her face just from the screeching, all twisted up with the vein pulsing in her forehead and the little mole by her eye twitching. Why did she always have to be such an ugly person? And I meant that personality wise. She always reached for anger first and I often wondered what her home life was like. Then I recalled Betty's warning. Maybe she really was just a jerk. So I hung up.

Strangely the phone didn't ring again. Maybe she was still yelling and hadn't realized she was yelling to herself yet, which made me smile as the doorbell rang.

I shrugged on my robe and stumbled bleary eyed to the door.

“Surprise!” yelled Vana as she held up a Katie May’s bag. “I brought breakfast. You look happy."

"Hey Vana. Bonnie was just yelling at me. Were we meeting this morning?" I’m sure my face looked appropriately puzzled.

"Um, no. I just felt you might need some cheering up. Why does Bonnie yelling make you happy?” she asked with eyebrows raised as she invited herself in.

"Haha, no. She was yelling so I hung up and she didn't call back. She might still be yelling to herself,” I answered yawning.

"Uh oh that can't be good."

"Probably not. She said I accused her of stealing my listing. Can you believe that?"

"Did you?"

"I did not. I have no proof," I added sadly. "Or I would have."

"So who did?"

"Huh? Interesting question," I replied as I walked to the kitchen and grabbed a couple plates and some napkins, setting them on the black granite island.

"I don't know why Bonnie gets in such a pickle with you," Vana commented as she sat on a bar stool. "We get along fine. I mean she does have an ego but that's not unusual among agents."

Sighing, I grabbed a couple glasses and the orange juice from the fridge. "I wish I knew. I've been nothing but nice to her but she always looks for every opportunity to bite my head off. Do you think she'll really report me to the board?"

"I don't know, but boy did she have questions about your date last night."

"What did you tell her?"

"Nothing. I didn't know anything to tell."

I joined Vana at the island and grabbed a container of bacon and eggs. "Honestly, I don't know what has happened to my life lately. My client's husband was almost dead, and then missing. The tow truck driver might have been murdered and Bonnie is out of control and then the Hotchkisses." I shook my head in frustration.

"What happened with the Hotchkisses? Wait. What murder?"

Taking a bite of eggs, I took a moment to answer, "I'm sorry, it's been such a long week. I met with the detective from Morecroft, who was much more informative than our local idiot. But I digress. I thought he was here investigating Carol but he was actually looking into Amos Belroy's death."

Vana was looking at me with a perplexed look on her face. "Who is Amos Belroy?"

Furrowing my brow, I replied, "the tow truck driver that fixed my car on Tuesday, which is strange according to Travis, because my car should have started on Thursday but it had a loose cable and didn't but he said Amos would never leave a cable loose."

Silence met my statement. Vana poured herself a sip of juice then casually asked, "who's Travis?"

Letting out a breath I hadn't realized I was holding, I replied, "That's what you got out of that?"

"Mmhmm. You're not answering."

"Travis is the detective from Morecroft, who came to investigate Amos's death. Apparently, they are friends and he swears Amos would never have faulty brakes." I swirled the juice in my glass, deliberately not looking in her direction.

"Is he cute?"

"Amos?"

"Don't be daft, you know who I mean."

"Well, maybe a little," I replied, remembering his gorgeous blue eyes. "Is it hot in here? Maybe I should turn the heater down," I added getting up.

"Sit down and tell me every little detail." Vana's voice was firm and she patted the chair cushion to emphasize her point.

Sighing, I dropped back down on the cushion and said, "Okay, he's gorgeous in a Brendan Fraser sort of way and he has the most beautiful blue eyes. And maybe," I added dragging it out, "I'm hoping he doesn't have to leave right away."

"Girl, that is awesome! It's about time you found someone interesting. I mean you're not getting any younger. When are you seeing him again."

Instead of replying I bit my lip, looking at Vana who looked back at me. "I don't know," I finally blurted out.

"You didn't ask, did you."

I blew my lips out in frustration. "I didn't ask. But he's investigating a possible murder. He should be here a while. Right?" I finished lamely. Vana reached out and patted my knee.

"If it's meant to be, it will happen. I truly believe that. So what's up with the Hotchkisses?"

This is what I loved about Vana. I could use her as a sounding board and she always saw everything so clearly.

"You got a second chance?" she exclaimed excitedly.

"Yes and no. She rescheduled and I missed the dog poop but I fell in the wet grass and muddied my pants, my car wouldn't start, I was too late to even go," I cried and then I really was crying.

"Is this my fault? Did I mess it up?"

Vana wrapped her arm around my shoulder. "No honey, of course it's not your fault. You just keep doing your best and your karma will find you."

"Thanks Vana, what would I ever do without you?"

"Probably curl up and die," she laughed. "I'm kidding, you know you would be just fine. Now go get in the shower and get ready for work. You wouldn't want to miss that karma when it comes knocking."

QUESTIONS

I was feeling immeasurably better by the time I got to the office. The office buzz filtered through my closed door. Everyone was busily at work. Everyone but me. I was sulking behind my desk when I was interrupted by a knock at the door. When I didn't answer Lucy poked her head in.

"Hey hun, you okay?" she asked concerned as she saw my face.

"I think Bonnie stole my listing appointment," I blurted out. There was no point in trying to hide it.

"That's a serious charge to make," frowned Lucy.

"That's why I'm not making it."

"You're not?"

"I can't. I have no proof but who else could have changed my appointment time? Mrs. Hotchkiss said 'she' and I don't have a she.'" Frustration filled my soul.

"Wait a minute, who's she?"

"Mrs. Hotchkiss said my assistant changed the appointment and referred to them as 'she.'"

"Oh, you poor, poor thing," sympathized Lucy. "I can't believe Bonnie had the gall to do that to you. You know she has a house recording tomorrow, I could accidentally misplace the file for a couple days."

"Thanks Lucy but you and I both know you would never compromise your integrity that way. I appreciate the thought though," I replied laughing.

"Yeah you're right but it felt good saying it," she laughed back. "You'll figure this out. You always do. Listen, I've got to make my rounds but I can come back for lunch."

"Thanks Lucy, lunch sounds good."

"Great, I'll see you at noon and see if Vana wants to come too."

"Will do."

Lucy was right. I do always figure things out. So I mailed my presentation to the Hotchkiss' house with an estimate of the listing price and kept my fingers crossed. Yes, I mailed it, not emailed it. I wanted her to physically hold it in her hands and look through it. All my calls to her went directly to voice mail, which was full. Was I blocked?

With my whole schedule shot to heck I focused on getting the ducks I did have control of in order.

"Hey Holly, how's my favorite boss?" I looked up from my computer to see Joe come in the door.

"Just awesome Joe, focusing on getting these deals closed."

"Well you're certainly chipper this morning."

"Shouldn't I be?"

"Yeees?" he answered, ending on a question as he shrugged off his jacket and hung it on the hook behind the door.

"How did the home inspection go this morning?" I threw it out casually as I glanced sideways at him.

"The inspector went by the Marples' house today and everything looks good. The buyers were there with Bonnie and they said no repair request. Bonnie didn't look happy about it though."

"Probably not. I transferred that listing to Vana but you can still follow up on the paperwork."

"You did what?" He looked a little shocked.

"I'm tired of dealing with Bonnie. I don't need the stress. Why does that surprise you?"

He stuttered trying to get out the words. "It, I, it's just, she didn't say anything? When did you decide this?"

"Last night. Vana is fine with it." And then, I don't know why, but I added, "you know what, just let Vana handle all the paperwork and everything. Just transfer it all over to her."

"Are you sure?"

"Yes, we have enough business as it is to deal with. She can handle it."

"I put your mail on the desk. Bonnie did say the Hajari's were going to accept the Makimoto offer."

"Well, that's good news. She must need money, like the rest of us," I forced a laugh.

"Hey, your friend that was at the Oates murder, does she have any more information?"

Joe froze for a moment like a deer caught in the headlights but then recovered quickly, sitting down at his desk. "She hasn't said anything to me." He bent his head to his computer and began typing.

"I'm just asking because a detective talked to me last night and he said there were no women techs working on that case."

"Do you think I lied?"

"No. I'm just confused because the police told Carol her husband was missing and that it was his friend that was killed. If it was Jerry, why wouldn't they have told her?"

"Maybe my friend got it wrong," he said defensively which puzzled me. This was a side of Joe I'd never seen before.He was usually so sunny. Was he capable of lying? Was he lying to me?

"I'm sure that's all it is," I replied soothingly. "I'm just so stressed right now and I need these deals to close. There's no time to deal with a murder right now. Poor Carol, she must be so stressed right now too."

He seemed to breathe a sigh of relief, "yeah, Carol, she seems like such a nice person. I hope you're right and he shows up soon." His mouth was saying the words but his eyes didn't match his tone. Something wasn't right with him.

"Joe, is everything okay with you? If you need anything you would let me know, right?"

"Everything is fine. Of course I would. It's just this whole murder thing and Bonnie is being such a pain."

"Okay, well let me know if you need anything. Or ask Vana. She seems to know how to handle Bonnie. I really appreciate everything you do. I don't know what I'd do without your help," I said smiling to reassure him. The truth was I would be lost without him. He was my right hand man and I would do anything to keep him happy.

"I have some errands to run," he said as he got to his feet, slid his computer into his bag and grabbed his jacket. "I'll check in with you later." He gave me a half smile as he opened the door.

"Hey Joe." He paused in the doorway with his hand on the knob. "The detective thought it was weird that my car wouldn't start right after the battery was replaced. You haven't seen anyone around my vehicle have you?"

"You think someone is messing with your car?" He asked, shocked. "You might check with Omar, he used to be a mechanic."

"Thanks, I didn't know," I said as he pulled the door closed behind him remembering Omar's surprised look. Left alone in the office, it was hard to concentrate on work. Questions kept pulling at me. I had to believe that Travis was telling the truth as he had no reason to lie which meant that Joe was hiding something. And there was Carol and the bathtub and the bone, was that really human? Where could it have come from? If it wasn't Jerry's, whose was it?

OMAR HAS A QUESTION

Well there was one question I could get an answer to. The one that really bothered me the most. Why did Betty ask about my husband? I grabbed my purse and opened the door and smacked right into Omar.

"Oh, I'm so sorry Omar."

"No, it's my fault. I was just about to knock." Really? He never knocked.

"Mmm, so Holly, I was wondering if you had some time later, if I could talk with you. I had something I wanted to ask you." He ran his hand through his hair awkwardly.

I'm pretty sure I knew what he wanted and it wasn't going to happen. "Well, I'm on my way out right now." His face kind of dropped and that part of me that insists on being polite to everyone kicked me. "Look, how about Monday?" I said, fishing my keys out of my purse and pulling my office door closed behind me.

"I was really hoping we could meet sooner. It's kind of important." On the other side of the office I could see Joe on the phone. He seemed agitated about something. Omar noticed my distraction and cleared his throat. "Um, yeah, Monday's fine. I'll see you then." Then added, "drive safe."

"Um, thanks. I will." What the heck was that about, drive safe? As I turned and walked away I swore he was staring at me but as I turned the corner and glanced back, the only one in my view was Joe.

Do you ever have a constant stream of thoughts going through your head that you can't shut off? That was my brain on the way home. Travis's comment about Amos not leaving a cable loose resonated through my brain. Did Omar do something to my car? And if so, why? Now that I knew he used to be a mechanic, did he have something to do with Amos's death? This new thought was pretty frightening as he worked with me. Maybe I shouldn't go into the office alone anymore. I'm usually a fairly good judge of character but I definitely didn't see that coming. Could Omar be a killer?

Was that Carol's truck Amos was referring to when he said he pulled one out because the battery was dead? Why would Carol get her truck stuck in the mud she knew was there and what was she doing in the dark with the lights on for so long, the battery died? Sure, she has animals, but I don't think they eat in the dark. Was she hiding something? Her husband's body? She did hesitate when I asked about the bones. Naw, it couldn't be her. For one thing, I don't think she's smart enough to pull off a murder and what would her motive be? What would Omar's motive be?

I pulled up the drive to Betty's house. The weeds were getting higher. I'd never noticed them before but the new tub planter was definitely getting devoured by the fluffy yellow heads of wild mustard surrounding it. Betty opened at my second loud knock with a sigh.

"Betty, why did you ask about my husband?" I couldn't help it, the words just burst from my lips without my thinking.

Betty's eyes opened wide at the force of the question. "Oh did I? Just curious, I suppose," she said brushing off my question.

"I had a feeling you meant something more,"

"Why would you think that?"

"The way you said it, like in that Star Trek movie when Picard is talking about the Borg and he says, 'but they won't stay on deck 9' or whatever it was."

"What are you talking about?" She creased her forehead in puzzlement.

"Oh never mind. It was just the inflection in the way you said it, like there was something more to know," my voice petered out helplessly. The wind was blowing through my jacket making me shiver. I wanted to scream in frustration. Taking a deep breath to calm down, I asked one more question.

"Betty, is everything okay with you? I noticed the weeds are growing and when I first listed Carol's house your yard just seemed so well kept." There was a touch of fear or anxiety in her eyes. Something was definitely up. "I'm not leaving until you tell me the truth. It's been a really long week and I can be as stubborn as a bull."

She shuffled her feet and looked down at the ground before answering in a low voice. "I have terminal cancer. Docs say I ain't got more than a week or two."

"But, but you seem so..." my voice trailed off into silence.

"I know, the doc said that sometimes people's bodies rally at the end, gives them a chance to put things in order."

"Does your sister know?" I asked in a quiet voice.

"No!" she said more forcefully than necessary. "And don't you go sayin' nuthin' either! She ruined my life just like she ruins everything. She can find out when I'm gone. Don't let her ruin yours any more. Promise me you'll stay away from her."

I looked at her helplessly, "I don't know about that, we have transactions together."

Betty took a moment to pull herself together. "I like you Holly, I really do. I didn't want to but when I met you I could just tell you were a good person. You're truthful and sincere. Promise me you won't ever trust her. She ruins people's lives."

Wow, that was really a change. I kind of felt cheated because I had just met Betty this week and now she was, in a sense, leaving me. "I like you too Betty. I promise, I won't ever trust her. I don't really understand why but I won't. There's always been something off about her and I trust you." Tears welled in my eyes. "If you need anything, you call me okay?"

In the doorway behind the screen, Betty just pressed her lips together and nodded her head. I made a mental note to hire someone to come weed whack her yard. If anyone asked, I would just say it was me going above and beyond for good will.

I shivered a little in the cold car as I started the engine, so I cranked the heat up as I drove away from the house. Why did I feel so melancholy? Was it the question about my husband? I tried not to think about it anymore. It had been ten long years. People tell you grieving is a process but I never realized it could be so long. You think you're fine and then one day out of the blue, something punches your emotions in the gut. Maybe if I hadn't moved, it would have been better. Maybe the pain would have ceased sooner if I was still living with all his things. Or maybe it just would have been worse.

That's the problem with 'what ifs,' there really is no answer.

A KATIE MAY'S CONSULTATION

Vana and Lucy's cars were already parked in the restaurant's lot as I pulled in. I gave my head a mental shake as I locked the car and straightened my clothes before entering the restaurant. No point in looking as unsettled as I felt.

A question had been burning in my brain all morning and I blurted it out as soon as I was seated.

"Vana, has your friend found out anything about the bone?" Of course I neglected to remember that Lucy knew nothing about it so we had to explain the whole story to her.

"Wow. That's crazy. Do you think it's Jerry?"

"No," answered Vana. "The bone belonged to a 30 year old man, so not Jerry."

"Well that's good." I breathed a sigh of relief. That definitely let Carol off the hook for using a bathtub to dissolve Jerry's remains. "But it still leaves the question, where is he? Carol still insists he's camping."

Katie May came by to drop off four glasses of wine. "You don't think it's too early for wine?" asked Lucy.

"It's never too early," stated Vana who had clearly ordered it when she got here.

Lucy raised her glass. "Here's to hoping Jerry shows up to sign his escrow paper work." We all clinked our glasses together.

"Who's the extra glass for?" I asked.

"Shelby, she'll be here soon."

Looking at the door, Lucy was the first to spot her and waved her arm to get her attention. We brought her up to date while waiting for our food.

"You have to take the bone to the authorities," she stated. As usual, always one for the rules.

"We can't. Carol is already under suspicion because her ex is missing."

"But Holly, what if she did kill him? We have to let the police know."

"Okay, Shel, but what if she didn't?" questioned Lucy. "We can't let an innocent woman go to jail."

I had to interject, "what if she's being framed? Isn't that what happens in those movies all the time?"

Vana, always the calm voice of reason decided for all of us. "Look. We'll just wait to see if Jerry shows up to sign his escrow papers. If he's fine and Carol is cleared then we'll tell the police. There's no point in causing a problem now. I mean we don't even know how long it was sitting there. And..." she added.

"Exactly," I said. "What if it was inside the dead pig? We don't even know where it came from. Maybe we should find that out first."

"Are you sure this is something you should even be investigating Holly? I mean, we have police for a reason," reasoned Shelby.

"Shelby I love you to death, but please, Carol is just a sweet ditzy client but she's my client and I need to help her."

"Okay fine, but if Jerry doesn't show up next week, you are calling the police."

"Yes. I promise."

"And..." Vana said again, pausing for dramatic effect.

Lucy squinted her eyes at Vana. "And, what?"

Vana took a moment to look at each one of us and then took a sip of wine. Shelby spoke first, clearly agitated. "Oh, come on Vi. Obviously there's something you want to share. Spill it."

Setting the glass down gently she clasped her hands on the table top, took a quick look around the restaurant and leaning closer to us whispered, "It's from a 30 year old man, who died 10,000 years ago."

"What!" we all exclaimed together, our eyes wide.

"Yes! My friend suspects it was stolen from a museum."

Shelby was the first to recover and ask the obvious question, "how the heck did it get in Carol's garage?"

MOVING DAY

I was at Carol's house later that evening so I was there when the police showed up. I wanted to stop by and update her in person so I could reassure her I believed in her innocence and to let her know how the transaction was going as she wanted to close before another house payment was due.

Her house was in various stages of packing in preparation for moving with a variety of filled and unfilled boxes throughout the rooms. "I see you're getting ready. What are you going to do with your animals?"

"I've sold them. They are going to be picked up next week and the dogs are going with me."

"Well that's good. The escrow is going fine, the home inspection was clear and the buyer's aren't asking for any repairs. We should be closed by next Friday," I explained as I walked through the living room. Carol had already taken everything down from her walls and placed them in a box on a stack of boxes. A framed photo in one caught my eye.

"I didn't know your husband like classic cars," I said picking it up for a closer look. "Isn't that a Pontiac LeMans GTO? Mike has one that looks just like this."

"Yes, it is. You know your cars." She walked over and pointed her finger at the car in the picture. "Jerry, he used to drive them when he had that series on television. Mike was his stunt man."

"Really," I said surprised. "I had no idea. What was the name of his show?"

"Rambling Man. Probably why it didn't last," she laughed. "He really loved those people that worked on it, they were like family to him." Carol took the photo from me and gazed at it. "Well, except for Mike," she said looking at it. "He never liked Mike, I don't know why."

"Has he lived down the street for very long?"

"I don't remember when he moved in. It's been a few years. I was actually surprised that he would want to live so close to Jerry when they don't get along." She set the picture back in the box. "Oh well, I guess you just do what you can when opportunity knocks."

How ironic then, that someone should knock at the door at that moment. We both laughed at the coincidence.

The laughter died away a moment later when Carol opened the door to find the police on her doorstep. An overweight middle-aged man in plain clothes was flanked by two officers in uniform.

"Carol Oates?"

"Yes, that's me. Did you find Jerry?"

"Mrs. Oates, my name is detective Moran," he said, conveniently ignoring the question. "You are under arrest for the murder of Lionel Hughes."

"Wait. What? Who, who is Lionel Hughes?" She questioned baffled.

"The man you killed in your husband's apartment," sneered Moran.

"I, I don't even know who that is! Holly?" Carol's voice rose into a frantic question as the police officer pulled out a pair of handcuffs.

"You thought it was your husband and snuck up behind him and bashed the unfortunate man in the back of the head," he finished triumphantly. "Just doing a neighbor a favor and you ended his life.

"My husband is camping!" she insisted hysterically. "Holly, you've got to help me. I didn't do this!"

I stepped forward to intercede. "Really detective Moran, don't you think she knows what her husband looks like from front and back?"

"Are you interfering with an investigation? I can arrest you too," he stated, glaring at me.

"I am not interfering," I stated emphatically. "Carol and Jerry are my clients. I have an interest in their well-being."

"Because of your precious commission?" Moran sneered.

I changed my attention to Carol from this insufferable man. "Don't worry Carol, I'll find out what's going on."

Carol turned her head to look back at me over her shoulder as two officers escorted her out the front door. "Please do. And see if Mike will feed my animals for me, please Holly." She looked like she was about to cry as Moran closed the door behind them and in my face to prevent me from following.

That man is so insufferable! I cut across the yard to Mike's house. His light was still trailing wires to the ground and the hose was still draped across the walk. The only thing different was the garage was closed. I made my way past all the detritus and knocked on the door which he answered with a smirk.

"Carol finally get arrested for offing her husband?"

"What? Why would you say that?" I asked shocked at his callousness.

"It's a small town. We all know what's going on and they weren't getting along." He stood there with his hands in his pockets with that smirk still on his face.

"Actually, no. She was arrested for killing someone named Lionel that was watching her husband's place." The smirk slipped from his face.

"Who's Lionel?" he asked just as puzzled as Carol was.

"I don't know, neither does she. Actually, I came over here because Carol was hoping you could take care of her animals until she gets out." I asked quite pleasantly because I really didn't want to do it myself. A dog is one thing but pigs and goats were quite another.

"Mike?" I prompted.

He shook his head and then shrugged his shoulders, "Yeah, sure, whatever she needs." He laughed. "That's what neighbors are for, right?"

Smiling, I answered back, "yes, thank you for that. I'll let Carol know not to worry." I started back across the yards when his voice called out halting me. "Hey, what happened to Jerry?"

I turned back with a frown. "What do you mean? I believe he's camping."

"Oh. Okay, thanks." Did he sound disappointed? Maybe I was imagining things. Maybe he liked Carol.

MEMORIES

It's Saturday morning and I'm depressed. Not even the sun shining in my kitchen window was helping today. Ginger must have felt my mood because she was lying next to my feet.

Betty is dying. I just met her and now she's going to be gone, permanently. I had no idea, she seemed so perky and full of life, I mean, now that I think about it, for a woman with animals, she was really very pale. The news was so crushing, like hearing someone died suddenly. Like in an accident. Like my husband. Why would a stranger I had never met ask me about my husband's death? There was just something so off about that that didn't sit right with me.

Sure Bonnie was off but Betty? I took a sip of my coffee and found it had gone cold. Careful not to step on Ginger, I eased out of the chair and went to refill my cup but instead found myself frozen as I contemplated my choices. There was no reason not to do it other than the fact that I'd put it off for ten years already. Sometimes procrastination is good, right?

No. I left the cup on the counter and returned to my bedroom, specifically the closet. Somewhere in the recesses may be an answer. I flipped on the light switch and knelt on the floor. When had I collected so much junk? I pulled out a box of sweaters I forgot I had, several board games that hadn't been played in years, a box of CD's, does anyone even use these anymore, and two pairs of sneakers that had seen better days, until I reached the last box. It was a pink floral filing box. I guess my sister wanted it to be cheery when she packed it with the remnants of a happier time.

Loss is a funny thing, sometimes a memory will fill you with happiness and other times it can make you cry. Looking at the box made me want to cry. I knew it was going to remind me of the last time I said goodbye to my husband. It was a morning like today. We had coffee in our sun filled kitchen and he gave me a kiss goodbye, hugged Chloe and walked out the door with a second cup in hand to drink on the drive. Normal, everyday routines that you take for granted.

Then there was a call at 5 p.m. to let me know he was on his way home, except he never arrived. The aftermath of that evening was in this box. I lifted it out from the back of the closet, my dresses brushing the top of my head. Taking the cover off, I found my sister had filed everything in file folders—photos, newspaper clippings, obituary, memorial service, police report. She is nothing if not thorough. I went to the newspaper clippings first because I figured all the rest would just make me cry and I wouldn't be able to read.

The first was from the 'Daily Sentinel' and was succinct.

Car accident kills local man. A man died when a car driven by a suspected drunk driver hit his vehicle as he rounded a curve in the road. A passenger in the oncoming car also died and the driver and two other passengers were hospitalized with serious injuries.

Follow up articles confirmed that the driver, Lana Wentworth, was indeed under the influence with an alcohol content three times the legal limit and went through the windshield as she also neglected to fasten her seatbelt. Her sister, Hope, was in the back seat and suffered minor injuries. The front seat passenger, Laura Wexler, died on impact and another unnamed passenger in the back seat suffered severe head trauma.

And that was it. The only strange thing was that the fourth occupant was never identified. Maybe they were under age at the time although the paper didn't say so. Odd but no point in surmising when there were no other facts.

I set that file down and braced myself to read the obituary as I had never actually read it before. My beloved husband was dead, I didn't need to read an obituary to know that. I pulled it out and gave a little laugh, my sister had put in the entire newspaper page.

My husband looked as handsome as ever in the photo. I reached out to touch the photo gently. It was one taken from our wedding nearly two decades before, we had been so happy.

As a tear crawled down my cheek I looked over the rest of the page. Laura's obit was the same day, another life destroyed by a bad choice. She looked so beautiful and young and left behind a husband. They should put the families pictures in the obits so people would remember the ones left behind that had to suffer the loss.

The tears were making it difficult to read. The only other picture was a middle aged woman who died unexpectedly. I don't know why I lingered on her picture as she wasn't someone I knew but, I don't know, there was just something familiar about her. Her name Hazel Brown didn't ring a bell either.

I don't know what Betty expected me to find, if she even did. Maybe I was reading something into an innocent question. Isn't that what older people do, ask intrusive questions?

This wasn't helping my mood. I put the box back and shoved everything back in front of it. It could stay there another ten years. I didn't care. I was fine before not knowing and I'll be fine again.

Reentering the kitchen, I grabbed a cup of hot coffee and snuggled on the couch with Ginger. Nothing soothes as much as a warm, soft canine. Flicking on the TV I scanned the channels for something lighthearted to watch, maybe I could find a cooking show.

Vana called not two minutes later. "Heeeyyy, I just wanted to remind you about our date tonight." Her tone was way too cheery for this moment.

I sniffled as I answered back, "Can we make it for another day? Sunday or next week even?"

Vana's emotion radar kicked into high gear. "What's wrong?" I never could get anything past her. "Are you sick?"

I just found out a friend is really ill, Carol got arrested and, and I went through the box."

"You did what now?" she asked, puzzled.

I took a deep breath before answering her. "My sister kept everything from that night in a box and I just looked at it." My throat felt like it was constricting and my nose became stuffed up suddenly.

"Oh. That box." Silence came from the other end of the line. "I'm coming over. I'll be there in twenty minutes." There was a click and the line went dead. I wanted to tell her I was fine, but really, I didn't think I could talk.

My best friend in the whole world showed up 19 minutes later with powdered sugar donuts an ice cold diet coke, and a hug. Sure it was really early on a Saturday morning but since when is it too early for diet coke and donuts?

I shoved a couple mini donuts in my mouth and swigged the diet coke before I felt able to talk. Vana looked at me and burst out laughing.

"What?" I asked, looking down at my clothes.

"You have powdered sugar all over your nose," she said as she reached over and brushed the particles off with her hand. "There, much better. Now tell me what's going on."

"Well, I got really bad news from a friend, a recent friend, but I can't tell you who it is. She only has a few weeks to live. And last night at Carol's house, they arrested her for the murder of Lionel, the guy who was staying at Jerry's house."

I took a deep breath and licked off my fingers giving Vana a moment to absorb the news. "You know the really weird part was when I went to her neighbor Mike's house to ask him to take care of her animals and he asked if she was finally getting arrested for killing her husband. I thought they were friends."

"Yeah, that's really a jerk move," added Vana.

"I thought so too. Plus Carol told me she and Jerry were divorcing on good terms. I can tell she still loves the guy. Do you want a donut?"

"No, thanks, those are all yours." Vana settled back on the couch. "So why did you open the box?"

Inhaling deeply and letting it out slowly, I began. "It was something Betty asked. She is Carol's neighbor. I went over to ask about the antique tub Carol gave her and she asked me how my husband died. It wasn't so much the question as the tone when she asked it." I paused for another sip of soda.

Vana pursed her lips in thought. "Did you find anything?"

"No. There were four people in the car that hit my husband. One died, one is institutionalized and two others were injured-one minor, one rather severely. It doesn't say what the injuries were." There was a niggling in my brain as if there was something important I should remember but it wouldn't surface. I sighed knowing that it might come later or not at all. Middle age is hard.

"What was that for?"

"What was what for?"

"The sigh."

I sighed again. "Because I feel like there's something important I should remember but I can't."

"Oh, okay. Well I called and rescheduled the date for next week, so don't worry about that." Vana bit her bottom lip, resting her chin on her clasped hands, thinking. When she gets like that I'm pretty sure it's not going to be something I like. She finally put her hands down in her lap. "How about I take a look at the box?"

My eyebrows shot up. "You want to look at the clippings?"

"Yes. Maybe I'll see something you missed. After all I never met your husband so it will just be information to me."

The lump in my throat wouldn't allow me to talk so I just nodded my head. She ended up taking the box with her with a promise to bring it back the next day. Standing on the doorstep, I watched as she walked to her car in my driveway. Watching the box leave gave me a feeling of loss. Vana stopped at the end of the walk with the box under her arm. "Hey. Why don't we get the girls together tomorrow after church and talk about Carol and Lionel. Maybe we can brainstorm something that will help them."

"That sounds good. Maybe it will get me out of this funk to feel like I'm actually doing something."

"Okay, see you then. At Tipsy's, they're having a band."

"Okay, Tipsy's. See you then."

A CALL TO TRAVIS

I put Ginger out back to use the facilities, admiring the green lawn and the border of flowers. Sure it's cliche to have a lawn surrounded by a border of flowers but I really enjoyed the contrast of the green grass to the bright colors of the flowers.

Reaching into the pocket of my robe, I pulled out my phone and tapped the button to call Travis. I mean Detective Smart. Maybe he would have some information that would help Carol and I could check into his progress with Amos. It was a relief when he agreed to meet me that afternoon at a small coffee shop in Morecroft.

Morecroft sits south of Appleby and is probably three times the size. While Appleby has more small business, Morecroft boasts several large chain grocery stores and restaurants. I had no problem finding the small coffee shop he suggested.

The coffee shop was really cute with pink chintz curtains and checkered tablecloths. Fresh flowers were on every table and it was old style with a cooking area behind the counter and small tables and chairs against the wall.

"This place is incredible," I said.

"Wait until you taste the food. The guys at the station give me a hard time about coming here but even they love the food," he responded, pulling out a chair for me to sit. Who even does that any more? He's definitely a keeper. You know, if I was looking for someone, which I'm not.

"I'm so glad you could come," he said, his blue eyes twinkling.

I set my purse by my feet and picked up the, you guessed it, pink menu. "I was actually going to say the same to you. It being Saturday and all."

Travis smiled and little butterflies swam up my insides.

"Welcome to Pinkies. Home of the pink burger, can I take your order please?" I looked up with a smile on my face at the waitress who had to be forty if she was a day.

"Isn't that from Good Burgers, the kids show?" I questioned.

She laughed. "Yes it is. My kids watch it constantly so I helped myself to it. I automatically feel like I should say it every time someone comes in."

Travis jumped in to say, "the burgers are awesome here."

"Well if you insist, I'll have the pink burger and a diet coke. Thanks. Uh, I don't really want it pink though just, you know, cooked all the way through."

"I'll have the same," said Travis handing the menu back to the waitress whose name tag read Clovis. "Thank you Clovis."

Travis then directed his gaze back to me which made my heart beat faster. Those gorgeous blue eyes. I needed a distraction. "Any luck with your Amos investigation?"

The question seemed to bother him and he began fiddling with his silverware. "No. Everyone seems to think I should just let it go but I can't. The coroner seems to think the head injury happened at the same time as the accident but I know Amos. I know it wasn't an accident. He was meticulous in his work."

Poor guy, he was determined to find out what happened and I couldn't even be bothered to look into the details of my husband's death.

"I'm so sorry. He seemed like such a nice guy."

"He was, he really was. You know he could have been a football star but he got hit really hard one time and that was it. No more football. He never really recovered from the head injury. That's why he went into the tow truck business, just wanted to help other people because of the help he received at the brain injury clinic."

Our order came and we fell silent while we devoured our lunch. I say devoured because I couldn't help myself. The burger was the best I'd ever had and the bun tasted homemade. Suddenly self conscious because of the juice running down my face, I surreptitiously wiped it off with the napkin causing Travis to laugh at me.

"Don't worry Holly, I've got the same problem," he said wiping his own face. A smile creased the corners of my lips involuntarily. He reminded me of a kid in a toy store. "So, what did you need to know?"

Oh, I needed to know a lot. For instance, was he single, dating anyone? But that's not what he meant. "My client Carol was arrested for the murder of Lionel, the guy in her husband's apartment. I know she didn't do it. Carol's not the brightest in the bunch but she loved her husband. She would never try to kill him."

"Let me guess, Moran arrested her."

"Yes. I just don't know how to help her. I mean I am not an investigator."

Leaning back in his chair, he considered the question. "Has Jerry showed up?"

"No, no contact yet. He's supposed to sign papers on Monday. I've got my fingers crossed," I said, holding up my hand and crossing the first two fingers.

"If she's innocent, there has to be another suspect. Who would have wanted to harm Jerry or Lionel?"

I thought back to what Carol had said. "I don't know Lionel at all but Carol said Jerry didn't like his neighbor Mike. I guess they used to work together on a TV series. She didn't know why he didn't like him."

"It's not my investigation and I don't normally step on people's toes, but with Moran investigating, she's going to need all the help she can get. He's really not a nice guy."

"Great."

"I'll do a little investigating and see what I can find out."

"Thanks. That would be awesome and not as Moran said, just because I want a commission," I said rolling my eyes. Another thought forced its way into my mind. Fumbling with my drink, I felt suddenly awkward. The words came reluctantly to my lips. "Since you're being so helpful, could you, I mean would you possibly..." This was ridiculous, I needed to just put on my big girl panties and ask. "Would you consider doing another favor for me. I shouldn't ask but..."

The concern showed in Travis's eyes as he answered. "What do you need?"

"Um, It's just a question a friend asked and I can't get it off my mind. It's my husband, Evan."

"I didn't realize you were married." Did he suddenly looked disappointed?

"I'm not. I mean I was. He died ten years ago in a traffic accident. A woman, drunk, ran his car off a cliff. That's why I went into real estate, it was something to do that would support my family without a degree but that had unlimited potential for income. I've always been great at selling people." The words all rambled together as I spoke, making me feel even more uncomfortable.

His clear blue eyes watched me steadily as I talked. "I'm sorry about your husband but what is it you need from me?"

"Is there any way you could take a look at the case file? I have clippings that my friend saved for me but I'm just wondering if there is any information that wasn't in the newspaper stories."

He leaned forward clasping his hands in front of his face and leaning his chin on them. "What are you looking for?"

"I don't know. A woman who doesn't know me or my husband was asking questions about his death and there was just something about the way she said it. I'm sorry, I really shouldn't ask you to do this. I just...I can't get it out of my head. Maybe it's all the deaths recently. I don't know. I'm sorry," I added, dropping my head to the table. This was all so frustrating. Now I was seeing conspiracies everywhere. The warmth of Travis's hand touching mine made me lift my head to meet his eyes.

"It's not a problem," he said quietly. "I can take a look. I lost my wife too. I understand what it's like to have questions." Hmm a widower like me. Stop it this is not something to be happy about!

"Thank you. Whenever you have time. It's not a priority." Now I was rambling. Just stop already.

Travis took out his phone, "what was his name?"

"Evan Holcraft. The accident was 10 years ago in Minford." Travis hesitated a second before putting the information into his phone. While he was doing that I sneakily handed the waitress my card to pay the bill.

MAGGIE LIKES DONUTS

Driving home through town I spotted someone I knew doing something they shouldn't so I stopped my car in the middle of the road.

"Maggie! Is that a donut in your mouth?" I yelled out the window. She stopped, panicked, like a deer in the headlights with her hand halfway to her mouth. "Sorry, I couldn't resist. I just have a question for you. When did you see the tow truck driver tromping in the mud?"

"Why do you ask?" Her eyes narrowed with suspicion.

"I think I may have known him."

"Why must have been early Sunday morning. I was walking my dog in the lane between our houses. I live on Oak Tree Hill."

"Behind the Oates," I interrupted.

"Yes, that's right. That ditzy Carol had her truck stuck in the back field. Serves her right driving along the road and leaving tracks to fill with water. Neighbors should be more respectful. That Carol is kind of cuckoo if you ask me," she said, twirling her fingers by her head. "You tell me how I'm supposed to walk my dog through mud like that. I've told her not to use that road," she snapped.

I grimaced at the tone. I guess it's hard to be nice when you're a grump. "Carol drove the truck?"

"I assume. It's her truck and her yard." She stated it as if it was the most common sense thing in the world and I was particularly dense. Okay, maybe she had a point this time.

"There's a road behind the houses?"

"Yeah, you can't really see it from Carol's place because of the bushes, but it's there. I tell them not to use it but nobody listens to me."

Well that was interesting. "Thank you Maggie. You've got a little powder on your face." I motioned with my hand to show her where it was. She attempted to brush it off as I rolled up the window and drove away but I could still hear her voice as she yelled at me, "We're not friends."

Arriving home, I grabbed Ginger and her leash then changed into my old jeans and a worn jacket I normally wouldn't be seen in public in and then grabbed a pair of rain boots for good measure before driving back out to Carol's place.

As I drove past Mike's house I noticed his driveway was wet again. How many times do you need to wash a car that stays in the garage? He hadn't fixed the lamp wires yet either. Maybe if he stopped washing his car, he could get something else done. Some people just were not safety conscious. I drove past and around the corner to the lane in between Maggie's and the residents on Carol's road.

Ginger was very excited to finally get some exercise in a location that wasn't home. Her excitement made me feel neglectful about her exercise. Sure, I had a fairly large backyard but it would probably do us both some good to go to a dog park. The road was fairly smooth except for the rut from a recent vehicle. Now dried out, they crumbled as I walked on them. Ginger left giant doggy prints behind as I followed the tracks to Carol's house.

Ginger and I walked the road past where Betty's house should be but I couldn't really tell because the view was blocked by trees and bushes. Walking further led us around a curve and up into the mountains. The physical part of me said 'no way' but the mental part of me encouraged me just a bit more. "The view will be fantastic," said my brain but my body was not so sure it was worth the effort. What am I even doing out here? I'm not a sleuth. This just shows the lengths I go for my clients. In for a penny, in for a pound except I think that's a British term. In for a dollar?

"Well, that's interesting." The tracks led up the hill but not into Carol's yard. They could have come from Mike's yard but he didn't have a workable vehicle. Mike was supposed to have moved the bathtub Saturday night but he never showed. Was it because the truck was stuck?

I turned Ginger, who was on the hunt for squirrels, around and looked back the way I had come in awe. The view was fantastic. It was just a little rise above the bushes but the whole valley could be seen with the east end of the lake in the distance. At this elevation I could see Betty, Carol's and Mike's houses. If the road in front of Maggie's house had this same view, selling a house there would be easy. Which begged the question, why would Jacob give up this view for Carol's house?

My thoughts were interrupted by my phone buzzing in my pocket. I fished it out to see it was Lucy calling.

"Hey Lucy, what's up?"

"We're going to Dagwood's Bar, want to come?"

I could hear Shelby in the background. "Tell her she has to come or we're coming to pick her up."

"Is that Shelby?"

"Yeah, we're in my car. We'll be at your house in a few minutes to get you," said Lucy.

"Tell her we're not leaving without her," yelled Shelby.

"Uh, I'm not home, I'm walking Ginger over at Carol's house."

"Okay, we'll be at your house in 20 minutes. Get your butt home."

"Oookay. I'll see you in 20 minutes." I disconnected the call. "Well Ginger I guess that's that for now huh?" She looked up at me with her cute doggy face, her little dots of eyebrows hopping up and down as she wagged her tail. Most likely because it was almost dinner time.

DAGWOOD'S BAR

Dagwood's Bar was a little dive in the center of town but it had a comfortable feel to it. The place was starting to get crowded on a Saturday night but we arrived to discover that Vana had snagged a table already.

I went over and gave her a hug, "You were right," she said. "This is way better than a blind date and an escape game."

"Girl, you were going on a date?" Exclaimed Shelby as she smacked my shoulder with her hand. "Do tell."

"Well, we were," jumped in Vana, "but I had to meet a client." She winked at me as she spoke from behind Shelby. I breathed a quick sigh of relief. I loved these ladies dearly but that was just something I wanted to keep private.

"Oh, hang on a minute," I said as I looked at my phone. I'd gotten a text from Omar. I really need to talk to you. Joe isn't who you think he is. That was pretty cryptic. I shoved the phone back into my pocket.

As we all sat down around the table, I noticed Lucy looking at Shelby weird. "What?" she exclaimed. "It's that time of the month and my boobs hurt. They just need a little fresh air, free from a restricting bra."

"Fine. Just don't go flaunting their freedom around. Someone might get hurt," said Lucy struggling not to laugh.

Shelby was what you called 'stacked' so their 'freedom' was pretty noticeable. "Yes, please, keep those puppies away from me. I would hate to accidentally get knocked out," I burst out laughing as I said it.

"Moving on," laughed Lucy.

We were enjoying ourselves until the cowboy came over. You know there's one in every bar that thinks he's God's gift to women. He looked to be in his thirties and much too old to be behaving like this. "Hey little darlin' can I buy you a drink?" He asked Shelby but his eyes definitely weren't looking at her face.

"Hey, honey, I don't think so," answered Shelby as she blatantly stared at his crotch.

"Why's that?" he asked. "What are you staring at?" he said as he looked down at his pants.

"If you're going to stare at my girls, I guess I can stare at your boys," she answered back snarkily. "I just can't help looking, the bulge, it's so...so..."

Our mouths all dropped open.

"See something you like?" he asked in a smug tone.

"It's just, it's so...small for a man with such a big ego." She spoke in too loud of a voice so everyone in the bar could hear. The smugness immediately dropped from his face as he looked around.

"Shelby!" gasped Lucy.

"You're not all that great yourself. Getting a little old and saggy aren't you?"

Shelby held up a finger. "That's one."

"You girls need to keep your friend in line," he snapped looking around at us.

"That's two. You're so typical," Shelby quipped back.

"Why you little b...," he began as his friends grabbed his arms and pulled him away.

"Sorry ladies," one of them said. "He's had too much to drink."

"And that's three," sighed Shelby.

"What are you talking about?" asked Vana aghast at her friend's behavior.

"Guys, they're all the same. First they stare, then they imply you're not good enough, tell your friends to keep you under control and then they threaten you when all of that fails. Every time." She shook her head sadly.

My female outrage kicked in. "You are exactly right. Sorry, Shelby, I was wrong to judge you. You let your girls shine. You have every right to give them a night out." Everyone at the table burst into peals of laughter. I looked to the door where the hapless man's friends were dragging him outside. "Don't bother coming back if you can't respect women!" I yelled out as the door shut behind him. Cheers erupted from the women in the bar.

A short time later the waitress showed up with four beers. "These are from the ladies. Your drinks are on the house tonight."

"What ladies?" we asked in unison.

"All the ladies. And thank you. He's been harassing women all night," she said to Shelby as she left.

"You're right," I said as I lifted my beer and held it in the center of the table. "This is definitely more entertaining than an escape room." We all clinked our glasses in a cheer.

An hour later and we were all in our happy places. Good company and cold beer did a lot to warm a person's heart. Until Bonnie showed up.

Bonnie charged up to our table and stood leaning too close with one hand on her hip and the other pointing at me.

"How dare you report me to the board," she said loudly, her voice quavering with anger. Although she was leaning over, she still managed to look as smug as ever as she looked down her nose at me. "I never stole your appointment. I. Don't. Need. Too. I am so much better than that. If you can't figure out your own life, that is not my problem. Maybe you should do a better job of training your employees." she added straightening and taking a deep breath.

"I have reported YOU to the board for slandering my good name. When I'm finished you won't have a license." She looked around the table at each one of us then spun on her heels and left without another word..

Lucy leaned over to me, "I thought you weren't reporting her?"

"I didn't."

"Well, then who did?"

"The only ones who even knew about it were the four of us."

"And Joe." commented Shelby.

"What?"

"Have you ever seen that meme going around that shows how men and women stand differently?"

"Um, yes?" I answered wondering where in the world Shelby was going with this.

"Look at Joe. What's up with that? It's like that kids show, one of these things doesn't belong," she answered, nodding towards the bar.

Looking over at the bar, Joe was lined up with five other guys. But where they were all standing with their feet apart, Joe had his together; something I would never have noticed.

Laughing, I responded, "What. Are you saying Joe is a, a girl?" The other girls looked as dumbfounded as I did.

"Wouldn't that explain everything?" she said defensively. "And maybe it would explain why he was laughing in the mirror just now."

"He was what?"

"Maybe one of the guys just told a joke," interjected Lucy as she tried to keep the peace.

"No, she's right," added Vana. "When Bonnie came in, everyone watched, except Joe. He kept his back to us the whole time."

"Like he knew what she was going to do," added Shelby. "Like how the criminal got caught in that television show because everyone looked at the victim except him."

"You guys are crazy. He's my assistant. He's been nothing but great to me."

"Except lately," said Vana. "Wait, hear me out," she added as I got ready to protest. "He knows everything that goes on. If he's really a girl, he could be the 'she' that changed your appointment."

The girls eyes all widened as the enormity of it all sank in. Lucy spoke first. "Did Joe cancel with the Hotchkisses? That would mean he was working with..."

"Bonnie?" asked Vana. "No way! Could he be?"

My head sank into my hands. "I really am jinxed," I groaned. "If he canceled my appointment, what else did he do? Did he make up that whole story about Jerry being dead just to sabotage my sale?"

"The real question is, 'what else did he do'?" Vana finished off her beer in one gulp. "You have to fire him."

Shelby glanced over to the bar. "I agree. You can't trust him. He has access to all your files, everything."

I suddenly remembered my text from Omar. "Omar texted me just before I got here and said Joe isn't who you think he is. Do you think he knows?"

Shelby suddenly rose from her seat. "I'm going to ask him."

"No!" I whisper yelled while grabbing her arm. "I'll take care of it. I need to make sure my files are secure first."

She sank back into her chair disgruntled. "Fine," she said as she rolled her eyes. "You're probably right."

"Girl, your hormones are not helping you tonight," admonished Vana. "Let's get you another drink before you kill someone."

"Not to change the subject, but I'm changing the subject," I began. "Did you know there's an old road behind Carol's place? It goes up the hill."

"Oh yeah, that old road," said Lucy. "It connects with another public road that goes roundabout aways then back into town. No one uses it anymore because it's so out of the way. And there's a cranky woman up there who yells at everyone who drives on it."

"Maggie," I said quietly as I sipped my beer.

"You know her?" Lucy frowned as she said it.

A laugh escaped me. "I met her in line at the grocery store when she called me fat. And then again a few more times. We've come to an understanding. But, as she says, 'we're not friends.'"

"Well okay then. You know, I think you could make friends with the devil," commented Lucy.

"Maybe, but not yet," I said. We all looked at each other and then said "Bonnie" together.

Unable to contain her laughter, Shelby sputtered beer on the table. Vana, Lucy and I all grabbed napkins to clean it up. "I'm so sorry," she gasped. "I just couldn't help myself. Could you imagine Holly and Bonnie as best buds?" She nearly fell on the floor in peals of laughter.

"That's it. You're cut off." I grabbed her beer and moved it all the way across the table. "Anyway. Maggie said a tow truck driver had to pull Carol's car out of the mud early Sunday morning. Apparently, she drove it down that old road and left ruts in it because of the rain. The thing is, Betty next door told Carol the pipes weren't buried deep enough and not to drive there. That's why she buried her animals there. Carol drove over the pipe breaking it and flooding her backyard, which is why the police were called. Why would she drive there knowing that?

"Plus, she had an old antique tub in her garage that her neighbor Mike was supposed to move to the neighbor's house Saturday night but he never showed. He moved it later AFTER borrowing Carol's truck. Does any of that make sense to you?"

"Wait? Antique bathtub?" asked Shelby.

"I know, *Breaking Bad*, it wasn't used for that, Tom said it would have ruined the tub. Although, Betty did say the finish was peeling so she used it as a planter instead." I blew out my lips in frustration.

"Lionel was killed Saturday night in Jerry's apartment. Don't you find that strange? That all this happened on Saturday night?" I questioned. Something about this bothered me deeply. "And they arrested Carol for Lionel's murder, but why not accuse Jerry? It was his place."

A man I didn't like the looks of approached the table. In his mid twenties, there was just an attitude about him that made me wary. "Um, excuse me."

"Yes, can we help you?"

He gave a cocky nod with his head in our direction. "You sure can. You can leave. If you can't control your friend, then you don't belong here. She's out of control and giving the other ladies ideas. Which quite frankly, my friends and I don't appreciate."

"It is beyond my comprehension that you would have the audacity to come over here and insult a group of women because they wish to have a little respect given to them. Furthermore, if my friends weren't 'controlling' their hormones,We don't control each other." I used finger quotes around the word control. "Maybe if you treated your ladies with the respect they deserve, there would be no ideas to get. Now get your self-righteous butt away from our table."

The guy looked dumbfounded. I couldn't tell if it was the big words or that a woman talked back to him.

"Yeah and we don't give a rat's ass about what your friends appreciate. Do you talk to your mother with that mouth?" Lucy questioned.

"We think what you did to that guy was disgraceful. Real women don't behave like that," he retorted.

"Real women?" Now my ire was up. I looked around at the ladies. "Are we faux women?"

Vana shrugged. "I'm real."

I looked back at the intruder. "Is this how your father raised you? Do you treat your mother as less than a person because she's a female? Oh, wait I get it." I shook my head as if in sudden understanding. "Your girls agree with us that women should be respected so now you can't 'control them.'"

Shelby stood up and grabbed Lucy's beer mug. "Hey ladies. I just want you to know that I respect all of you. Even the one who's dating this misogynistic jerk." She stumbled a little as she went to sit back down, then stood upright again suddenly and looked around the room. "My sympathies to whoever that is."

By this time the guy was just fuming and his face was red. I sort of felt sorry for all the guys in the bar this evening but my mama bear was in full mode as was Vana's.

She stood up all five foot four inches of her and said authoritatively, "I really think you should leave. Now." He couldn't see it, but all of the women in the bar had come to stand behind him while we were talking.

"I'll leave when I want to. You have no right to talk to me or any other man like that. Where would you be if you didn't have a guy to take care of you?" he sneered back. Well he sneered until a woman tapped him on the shoulder. I assumed it was the one he came with because she had been glaring at him for some time now.

He had shrugged her off a few times but now he turned around thoroughly pissed off. "What?!"

The girl pressed forward so he backed uncomfortably into the table. "Don't ever ask me out again you creepy little jerk!" She enunciated each word with a finger poke to his chest.

He pressed his lips together in anger, starting to speak, but thinking better of it. "I'm out of here. I don't need this grief." He pushed his way through the women to the door. "Don't ever expect to see me in here again," he yelled back over his shoulder.

The women all whooped with their fists in the air. "Thank you," the girl said. "I'm Amanda and I'm glad I saw who he really is tonight. I don't need to waste my time on grief like that."

"Well, tonight took an unexpected turn. Shelby, I'm sorry for taking your beer away," I said as I slid it back to her. "Go ahead and drink up and let your hormones fly. I shouldn't have said what I did just because I was uncomfortable."

"That's okay, Hol, I was a little out of control."

Vana raised her eyebrows. "A little?" She said then buried her face in her beer mug.

"Ladies, if you want to continue this, we can go to my house. I have plenty of room for a sleep over," I offered. They all declined but the bartender offered to see us to our cars, just in case a disgruntled boyfriend was still around. Fortunately, they had all gone home and we did the same.

VISITING A FRIEND

Sunday morning dawned bright and clear. Vana would be at church which left me to my own devices so I geared myself up for another visit to Betty and this time I wasn't leaving without an answer.

Pulling up to her house, I noticed the weeds had finally been taken care of and the tub was shining bright in the morning light. Knocking on the door brought no response so, feeling rather foolish, I took to peering into the windows.

"She's not home."

I turned to the voice and saw Carol in her doorway. "I'm so happy to see you. Did the police let you go?" She looked terrible as if she hadn't slept at all.

"I was able to post bail based on my house closing soon. The bondsman took pity on me." She shook her head sadly and a tear trailed down her cheek. "I just hope that Jerry's okay or I'll lose my house too. How did this happen? One day everything is fine and then bam! It all goes haywire."

Unbidden, the memory of the police telling me my husband was gone popped into my head. I had to take a few breaths before I could speak. "I'm so sorry Carol. Do you need anything?"

"Would you like some coffee?" she asked. "I mean it would be so nice to just talk for a few minutes."

"Of course Carol, I missed my coffee myself this morning. A cup would be wonderful," I said as I hurried across Betty's lawn. "Do you know where Betty is? Isn't it awful early for her to be out?"

"She wasn't here yesterday when I got home," she replied.

Now I was beginning to worry. Did something happen? Was she in the hospital? I needed to stop thinking bad thoughts just because I knew she was ill. She could be visiting a friend or any number of non hazardous things. Focusing on Carol, I offered to make the coffee. As her kitchen window looked out onto the back yard, I found myself looking across into Betty's yard to see if I could spot anything amiss.

I brought the two mugs of coffee back into the living room where Carol fortunately, still had her couch. "I see you've pretty much got your house packed up. What are you going to do if you can't leave town?"

"I'm going to get a hotel room for a while. Hopefully, this won't go on too long. They can't convict you if you didn't do it right?" She looked at me hopefully, her voice a little shaky as if trying to convince herself of the truth.

I opened my mouth to answer when someone banged on the door so hard, we both jumped.

"Were you expecting someone?" I asked, walking to the door as Carol looked like a deer in the headlights.

"I can't take any more surprises, would you please?"

Glancing through the curtain in the front window revealed an angry, middle-aged woman beating on the door with her fists. Instead of opening the door, I yelled through it. "Can I help you?"

"You let me in right now you boyfriend killer!" she screamed. Seeing as how it was barely 8 am Sunday morning, I opened the door and the woman stumbled through it, landing on the floor. Carol scooched herself all the way up on to the couch and sat with her knees in front of her face as if that would protect her.

Extending my hand to the woman on the floor I said, "Hello, my name is Holly and I'm Carol's agent and friend. And you are?"

She slapped my hand away and angrily declared, I'm Gloria and she," she said pointing at Carol, "killed my poor Lionel." She then collapsed in sobs.

"Carol, please go get Gloria a cup of coffee, I think she needs one. Now," I added as she wasn't moving. I needed to keep them separated until I could find out what was going on.

"Gloria, I heard about Lionel and I'm really sorry but Carol didn't do it. Detective Moran is just a little too eager to solve his case the easiest way he can. Why don't you come sit next to me on the couch and you can tell me what you know," I added, patting the seat next to me.

Reluctantly she got up off the floor, swiping at her eyes as she made her way to me. "Lionel, he was watching Jerry's house for him while he was camping, you know, watering his plants and such. Someone snuck up behind him and bashed him over the head. My poor Lionel," she cried, dissolving into tears again. "I came by to see him and found him on the floor."

"You found him?"

"Yes, I called the po..police." A woman told Joe that Jerry was dead.

"Do you know someone named Joe?"

"Joanna? Yeah, my friend's sister. I told her Lionel was gone." She took the coffee and tissues that Carol brought her. "Thank you. I, I'm sorry I yelled at you."

"It's okay," Carol responded, taking the moment to walk all the way across the room from Gloria ensuring stacks of boxes remained between them. I couldn't blame her as I would have probably done the same.

A bright shining light, a moment of clarity came to me and I turned to Carol to confirm it.

"Carol, I need a little clarification. You said you were getting divorced because your husband would just randomly take off and leave you alone."

"He does."

"Isn't it really because he's gay?"

Shock passed over Carol's face and she felt behind her for a chair and sat down as if her legs couldn't hold her up. "How did you find out?" she whispered through her hands.

"I saw a co-worker at a gay bar and something clicked just now. I couldn't even tell you what it was. Why did you lie to me?"

"I was afraid you would think I was guilty and I didn't do it!"

"Better not let Detective Moran find out. He'll consider that a motive for sure." I tapped my finger against my lip as I tried to think what to do. This information certainly put Carol in more of a predicament and now I had two distraught women and still no answers. Well, I had confirmation of one. My phone rang interrupting my thoughts.

"Betty!" I exclaimed as I answered.

"Yes, well, you don't have to be so excited about it. Mike called and told me there was a nosy woman peeking in my windows so I assumed it was you. Well, I'm in the hospital. I'm fine!" she added quickly before I could ask a question. "I just have a touch of a cold but, well, you know, so I didn't want to take any chances."

Well, that was quite the explanation. Feeling immensely relieved I got her room number and told her I would be stopping by and there was no use protesting. Clicking off I looked at the two ladies.

"Are you two going to be okay together?" They looked at each other before responding. Gloria began first.

"I just want to say that I'm sorry again," she looked at Carol. "I can see that you're not one to kill someone and Jerry spoke so highly of you."

"Thank you and I'm really sorry about Lionel. I didn't know him but if he was a friend of Jerry's he had to be a good guy. Jerry only hangs around with the best people." She moved over to the couch as she was speaking and sat down next to Gloria. "Maybe we should add a little extra something to our coffee and talk?"

"That's my cue to go. Betty's in the hospital with a bit of a cold, you know at her age, you can't take any chances. I'm just going to go by and take her some flowers. Call me if you need anything."

HOSPITAL VISIT

At the hospital, I was surprised by Travis in the hall outside Betty's door. A smile creased my face at the sight of him.

"Do you know Betty?" I asked him.

"Betty?" He looked puzzled.

"She's Carol's neighbor. I met her while I was door knocking. She's a bit of a character actually. You're right outside her door," I said, indicating the hospital room number on the wall. Travis looked at me strangely then shook his head.

"No. I was just here trying to get more information on Amos."

"Did you find anything new?"

"Not yet. I was just on my way to get the autopsy report but they said it wouldn't be ready for a few more days. Hey, I've got to run but I'll call you later okay?"

"Yeah, sure." Watching him walk down the hallway left my feelings in a jumble. Was I actually sad he didn't stay?

Betty's tiny body was surrounded by pillows propping her up in the hospital bed.

"Who was that man you were talking to in the hallway?" she asked as she took the flowers. "They smell delightful. Thank you."

Looking back to the hall I frowned. "Do you mean Travis?"

"The nice looking one."

"Travis Smart, he's a detective from Morecroft. He's looking into the death of his friend, Amos."

"Amos Belroy? I heard about that on the news. Such a nice man. He came by Sunday morning to pull Carol's truck out of the mud."

"Mike said it was Sunday night."

"Well Mike's an idiot. It was early Sunday morning because I was gone Sunday by 7 am. Carol said she would feed the cows for me."

"Huh. Well how are you feeling? I was so worried when you weren't home."

A smile crept over Betty's face against her will. "Awe look at you all worried about little old me." She played with the flowers in her lap. "You know, I was wrong about you. You really are a nice person and I've met so few of them in my life."

"Thank you and I'm so sorry to hear that. It takes so little to be a nice person. Well, usually," I added thinking of her sister. "What is your sister's problem anyway? I can't imagine you having to grow up with her."

Betty was suddenly too interested in the flowers. It was several moments before she spoke and I let her have her time. I've learned that some times it's best to let the silence stretch to get people to speak.

"Life didn't turn out the way she wanted it to. It...she." She stopped talking, biting the inside of her cheek as if figuring out what she wanted to say. "Her choices aren't mine. She, she has something wrong inside. Even when she was little...she made...bad decisions and maybe the repercussions were worse than she deserved but sometimes I just don't know. What I do know is I don't want to spend my time talking about her. Please let's not bring her up again?" She looked at me hopefully and maybe with a little desperation in her eyes.

"I'm sorry Betty, I won't talk about her again." I really, really wanted to talk to her about my husband but this wasn't the time for that either. Grudgingly, I accepted that the questions would have to wait.

"I should probably go and let you get your rest. I'll call later and check in on you and," I paused dramatically. "You let me know what food I can sneak in here for you."

Betty beamed. "Anything from Katie May's, you know this hospital food is terrible."

Leaving the hospital left me surprisingly happy. Betty's crankiness somehow seemed to cheer me up. Arriving home I found a vase of flowers on my doorstep with a note from my daughter thanking me for being a great mom. I took the flowers inside and then spent the rest of the afternoon relaxing with Ginger and talking to my granddaughter on the phone.

OMAR

It's just another rainy Monday, ooo ooo. The lyrics to the song kept repeating through my head. If they were even correct. It was raining cats and dogs today but my office was a nice quiet respite from the wet. I love rainy days. Everything looks brighter and greener after a rain and it smells so fresh. Here's hoping it bolsters me for what's to come today.

I'd barely sat down at my desk when Omar poked his head in the door.

"I see you're busy, I'll come back."

"No, no, come on in." Curiously I was in a peaceful, generous mood today and I knew he would just keep coming back if I didn't talk to him.

"Omar, Joe told me you're a mechanic. Would you know any reason why my car wouldn't start the other day?"

His eyes opened wide as he exclaimed, "no, why would I?"

"I'm not accusing you of anything. I was just looking for advice. Why are you so defensive?" I questioned back."

"I didn't know you were having problems with your car," he snapped back.

"No? You were there the other day when it wouldn't start." I stated.

He was wringing his hands and his face had gone red. I had a sneaking suspicion he was about to cry, which was weird. "I, I just wanted to see if you would mentor me but every time I tried to ask, you were busy. My business isn't going well and you seem to always be able to pull your deals together when they fall apart."

Omar hung his head.

"Oh." Shame cut through me like a knife. I had badly misjudged him. "I'm sorry, it's just that the detective looking into Amos's death told me he would never leave a battery cable loose."

"Amos? Amos Belroy?"

"Yeah, that was him."

"Was? What happened to him?"

"He died Tuesday afternoon when the brakes failed on his truck."

"But you said a detective?"

"Yeah, he doesn't believe it was an accident.

"There's no way it was an accident, no way Amos's brakes would have failed. He was meticulous. We worked together for a while. He used to play football, but got hit once really hard in high school and suffered a brain injury. That's why he became a tow truck driver."

"Oh, Omar, I'm so sorry."

"I've also been trying to tell you that Joe...well it probably isn't my place to say but, he's been lying to you."

"What do you mean?"

"I saw him meet with Bonnie and, and..."

"He's really a girl."

Omar looked up and his eyes widened. "You knew?"

"I just found out. How did you know?"

"I saw him at a party organized by a dating site last year. I don't think he remembers me though. He was talking to someone about transitioning."

"Huh." Well that was a revelation. "You saw him meet with Bonnie?"

"Yeah. I should have said something," he added sheepishly. "That woman has something wrong with her."

"Why do you say that?"

He shrugged his shoulders. "Just a feeling. Well, I guess, I'll go." He reached for the door handle looking like a dog that just got kicked by its owner.

"Omar wait! I would love to help you with your transactions. Let's set up a time next week to go over your files." As the words left my mouth, he instantly brightened.

"Thank you Holly. I'll even split them with you if you want. I just need to get something closed."

"That's not necessary," I smiled to put him at ease. "Let's just get them closed."

Opening the door to leave revealed Vana standing there about to knock. "Hello Omar, everything okay?"

Omar smiled, "Everything is fine now. Thanks, have a great day." He passed by her and she came in and sat on my small couch.

"I just had a most interesting conversation with Omar."

"The lurker?"

"I completely misunderstood him. He just needs help with his transactions and he's definitely not interested in me."

"Well, that's good to know but what I don't understand is why Joe would work with Bonnie. Why not just go work for her? Why all the underhandedness?"

"That's a good question Vana, and one I hope to find an answer to. I expect him in shortly and boy is he in for a surprise.

While we waited, I called my local MLS board just to ease my mind.

Hello Lydia, Bonnie is accusing me of reporting her to the board and I just wanted to clear things up. There was silence on the line as I explained everything to Lydia, the board president.

Well this is all news to me. Unfortunately, if someone did complain, it would be confidential. As far as Bonnie goes, there's nothing we can do about it as there's no proof. While if she did do it, it would certainly be unethical but she hasn't broken any laws. And as you said, you don't know for sure that it was her. If you do get proof that she is deliberately interfering with your business, well then we can possibly fine her. As far as her accusing you of reporting her, there are no reports against her, so I'll try and calm her down if I see her."

It was as I expected, but I still felt a little disappointed. "Thank you Lydia. I don't want to cause any trouble but I did want to let you know what she said, just in case she pushes the issue. Thank you for listening to my problems."

"No problem at all. You have a good day."

As I disconnected the call, I turned to Vana. "Well, you heard. What do you think of that?"

"I think Joe told her what you said and she jumped to conclusions. And I think, after you fire Joe, your life will be much better."

Joe showed up an hour later in high spirits. He hung up his coat and sat at his computer. I wanted to give him a few moments.

"Hi, I'm Jerry Oates," said a deep voice from the doorway. "Are you Holly?" The man in the doorway was big and burly but in a teddy bear sort of way.

"Yes, Mr. Oates, come in. I'm so glad to see you. This is my assistant Joe." Was it my imagination or did Joe look a little pale?

"Call me Jerry. I just wanted to come by and say thank you for helping my wife. It's been so traumatic for her. I don't know why anyone would accuse her of that. I mean our divorce is amicable, we're not even fighting over anything. I really was camping. There's just no cell reception up there and Carol has never been there so she couldn't give accurate directions."

I smiled at him. "That's what Carol said too. I'm so glad you are okay. I'm really sorry about the break in at your house. Have the police found out anything?"

Jerry hung his head. "No. They think it was a robbery gone wrong but nothing was taken so how could it be a robbery? Poor guy, he was just watching my house for me while I was gone. I feel so bad, I knew him for 20 years," he said in a voice close to tears.

I had never met Jerry before but I instantly liked him. "It's not your fault, there probably wasn't anything you could have done," I said knowing they were just words and weren't going to make him feel any less guilty.

"Thanks, I appreciate that. I signed all the paperwork and escrow has my bank information so I guess that's it." His eyes roamed the office as he spoke. "Thanks again for everything. I'd stay longer but I've got a car to buy."

"Thank you for coming by and good luck with your car purchase." I extended my hand for a quick shake after which he left, closing the door quietly behind him.

"Well, that answers the Oates question, Joe. Hey, why did your friend think he was dead?" I asked, looking at him, which is why I didn't miss the weird look on his face.

"I don't know," he said, shaking his head. "I guess she just got the information wrong."

"Are you okay, Joe? You don't look well."

"No, I'm fine."

I yawned, it had been a long night after all. I settled back, making myself comfortable in my chair and letting Joe get settled at his desk. Out of the corner of my eye I could see him changing web pages rapidly. After letting him suffer for several minutes, I finally sprung a question at him. "Why did you change my appointment with the Hotchkisses Joe? I know you did. What I don't know is why you did it."

His eyes widened in shock. "Yes. I know it was you. When I told you Bonnie cheated me out of my listing, you never asked what she did. Because you already knew because you did it."

"But I...I didn't.." he stammered, then suddenly got angry. "I wouldn't. Maybe if you didn't spend so much time watching your granddaughter, you would remember things better."

And it was at that moment that I realized something. "You know what Joe? I like watching my granddaughter whenever it is. It's an unexpected pleasure that always brightens my day. And my daughter does appreciate me. You are right though. Sometimes it does interfere with my work and so I'm going to schedule one day a week to just do fun things with her. That will give me a break and also Penelope and perhaps she won't have so many unexpected requests. Yes. That's exactly what I'm going to do. Thank you Joe for helping me work that out."

I paused for dramatic effect.

"You may have noticed you can't log in to any of my accounts. I spent last night changing all of my passwords. He stared at me, chewing on his lip. Probably trying to figure out just exactly what I knew.

"Joe." It was just the one word but he was looking at me like a deer in the headlights. "You didn't think the whole Jerry dead thing through very well did you?"

"Wha, what do you mean?"

I let out a long slow breath to calm myself and began again. "At Carol's that first Monday, you said they found Jerry's body in his house but they hadn't. It was Lionel, and Jerry really was camping. What did you think you were going to accomplish by making that lie? You had to know the truth would come out fairly quickly."

I could see the wheels turning in his head as he sought to come up with an explanation but I cut him off.

"It's okay, Joe. I know the truth. Bonnie told you to interfere with my business. What I don't know is why. Why would you do that Joe? I thought of you as a friend."

Anger crossed Joe's face again. "Bonnie is right. You don't deserve to be successful. You believe every sucker's sad story."

"Does that include you Joe? I believed in you."

The disgruntled look on his face showed he hadn't really thought this through. Just like all of his other plans he hadn't thought through. "The reason I'm successful and you're not, is because I do think things through," I continued. "If Jerry was dead that would have canceled my transaction but he isn't and that would never have been difficult to prove. Changing my appointment with the Hotchkiss's was actually pretty good but that's where you gave yourself away. Bonnie denied it. You never had a female friend with the police."

Joe stood there fiddling with his fingers.

"What you did have was your sister's friend who told you that her boyfriend, Lionel, had been killed in Jerry's house."

Now his face was white. "I really had high hopes for you Joe. You're the best assistant I've ever had but you crossed several lines. I'm so disappointed in you. You're fired Joe. Please take your things and leave. And Joe, Bonnie hasn't been doing you any favors."

Compressing his lips, he gave a brief nod, then gathered his things and left. There was no point in asking for his key back as he could have made copies and besides, I had already called the locksmith to have the lock changed.

Vana came back in. "That seems like it went okay," she said.

"Yeah," I sighed. "I really liked him."

"Look on the bright side. Jerry's alive and your escrow is going to close."

I had to laugh. Vana always looked on the bright side.

Despite what Vana said, I called escrow myself just to double check and Diana assured me that he had signed and the file was funding today and recording tomorrow which was great news for me, Jerry and Carol.

A FRIENDLY VISIT

Lucy came by around noon to 'check if I needed anything from her company' which was really just a ruse to chat. Vana saw her stop by and joined us once again, locking the door behind her. Lucy just looked at her with her eyebrows raised.

Vana stared back innocently. "What? I'm just trying to keep the riff raff out while we discuss title options. Okay, fine! I want to know what the update is on the Carol murder investigation and that cute detective. That is why you're here, isn't it?"

Lucy plopped on the couch. "Yes it is." She bobbled her head as she answered. "So what's going on?"

"Welp, Jerry came back and signed all his paperwork. He really was on a camping trip. He and Carol are divorcing because he's gay."

"Ooo did he leave her for another man? That'll make any woman want to kill him."

"No he did not. He's like a big teddy bear, there's no way to dislike that guy."

Lucy looked disappointed. "Well, then who did it? Did Jerry kill Lionel out of jealousy?"

"I don't know and no. Lionel's girlfriend, Gloria, showed up at Carol's house Sunday morning extremely distraught. I thought she wanted to kill Carol. I don't think either of the women did it. I don't think they're capable of it and what's the motive?"

"Women are good at faking," cut in Vana.

"That is true," I replied.

"Well, who does that leave?"

Pressing my lips together, I thought about it. Who did that leave? "There's the neighbor Mike. Carol said Jerry didn't like him but she didn't know why and I don't think he likes Jerry either. Omar knew Amos, said he was in rehab for a while for a head injury. Mike's on disability for a head injury from work. Do you think they knew each other?"

"Wait, wait, wait," Vana held up her finger and wagged it in our faces. "You said Omar met Jerry at a party for a dating site and saw Joe there." She stopped and gave us a moment to think about her statement.

This time my eyes were big. "Are you saying you think Omar is?" Vana just nodded her head.

"Oh, shoot, guess I really misjudged him."

Vana just rolled her eyes. "Yup. Guess that's making you rethink my dating selections, mmhmm."

"Um. Still no." Putting my elbows on my desk I leaned my chin on my clasped hands. "Hmm, so we have three questions. Who killed Amos and why? Who killed Lionel and Why? And why is Bonnie out to get me?" I ticked the items off on my fingers as I recounted them.

"One. Lionel was killed Saturday night. Two. Mike was supposed to move Carol's bathtub for Betty Saturday night but never showed. Instead he said he was giving a drone demonstration to the scouts which fits, because Betty said he was shining lights in her window and disturbing her cows."

I saw Lucy frowning. "What?"

"It's just that drone lights aren't very bright, I don't know if they would shine in a window enough to bother someone. I could see headlights bothering her but the cows are in back right? And how many cows does she even have? Those yards aren't huge."

"I don't know, I've never actually seen them. We're getting side tracked. The drones could have flown too low and bothered the, how ever many cows she has, except she specifically mentioned the lights." I tapped my fingers against my lips while I contemplated the issue.

"Three. Amos was killed Tuesday afternoon, shortly after putting a battery in my car. He said he had to tow a truck out of someone's yard Sunday morning. Maggie said she saw a tow truck in Carol's yard 'tromping' around in the mud, it had to be Amos but did he know Mike or Lionel? Travis and Omar both knew him."

Vana pulled out a paper and began documenting the details. "So Mike could have killed Lionel thinking it was Jerry, but why?" she questioned. "You need to find out what the disagreement was about."

"I have to find out?" I protested. "I'm not a detective. Lucy's more of a detective than I am."

"Oh hold on now," jumped in Lucy. "I just investigate title issues. Not dead people. Vana's the one with the sciencey friend."

Vana cleared her throat. "I think we're getting off track here. Holly really needs to find the connection between Lionel and Amos."

"Let's explore that," I said sarcastically. "Jerry knew Lionel. Who else did? Does Jerry know Amos? Did the two ladies kill them both?" Even as I said it I knew it wasn't true but did Jerry know Amos? Was there a connection between them?

"Why are you smiling?" asked Lucy.

"Am I?" I asked as I realized I was. "Okay, well, I think I might be able to get some answers from Detective Smart. I'll talk to him and see if he's free."

"She went on a date with him," Vana added smugly.

"I did not go on a date with him, he was investigating his friend's death."

"At Tipsy's."

"Sounds like a date location to me," Lucy commented. "Definitely go talk to him for information," she added using finger quotes around information.

TRAVIS HAS INFORMATION

In the end I didn't have to call Travis as he called me and said he had information for me. We made plans to meet in Morecroft as there were way too many prying eyes in town for my comfort. We went back to the little pink coffee shop which made a pretty cheery location to discuss murder.

Travis was already in a booth when I arrived and looked rather uncomfortable. What could he have found out? Tension instantly filled me as I watched him twisting his neck as he adjusted the collar on his shirt. Sliding into the booth across from him I smiled nervously.

"You said you have information? Is it about Carol?"

Travis took a deep breath and leaned back in the booth. "Yes and no."

"Huh?"

"When I saw you in the hospital I was following up on a tip about your husband's death."

Now I was the nervous one and I fiddled with the glass of water on the table. "What was the tip?"

"Someone told me the woman who was responsible for the accident lived out here."

"In Appleby? That's disconcerting." How did I feel about that? Is this what Betty wanted me to know? "I mean, I don't know what they look like. Have I met them? Am I friends with the woman who killed my husband? Why, why didn't I check into this more?"

Travis reached across the table and grabbed my hand which I had curled into a tight fist. "Hey, it's okay. We all react differently when we lose someone and it's not like you knew what the future would be."

I knew he was just trying to comfort me but I was angry now and felt violated that the person who caused my husband's death might know me, but I had no idea who they were. My mouth was suddenly dry and my tongue wouldn't work to speak. How could I betray my husband this way?

With tears threatening to fall from my eyes, I pulled my hand back from Travis's. "I need to go. I'm sorry." Anger made me stand up from the table and take a step to the door before I could control myself. Standing by the table with my hands in fists by my side, I asked one more question. "Do you know who she is?"

Travis let out a deep breath. "No. She changed her name and I haven't been able to find out what the new name is. I'll keep trying." He walked around the table to me and put his hand on my shoulder. "Listen, I know this is upsetting Holly, and I need to tell you..."

"What about Carol," I said, cutting him off. "Did you find anything that will help her?"

He made as if to speak, then changed his mind and shook his head. "Moran doesn't have any evidence against her. Her truck was stuck in her backyard Saturday night, there's no tracks leaving her yard and she has no other vehicles." He took a deep breath. "But he's convinced she's guilty. I'm sorry but I can't look into it more. I have to find out who killed Amos. I can't let a murderer go free.

"Maybe Amos' death was just an accident," I said quietly.

"It wasn't."

I threw up my hands, letting my frustration get the best of me. "Maybe Bonnie killed Amos."

Travis stared at me. "What earthly reason would Bonnie have to kill Travis?"

"Oh, I don't know. Why would Carol kill Lionel? Maybe there are no answers. I just need to clear Carol."

"That's what this is really all about, isn't it," he said angrily. "Closing the deal. You're really all about the end result aren't you?"

His words cut deep. Was I? "I'm a nice person!" I choked out between sobs. "I have to go."

I turned and left him standing there.

On my way home, I rang Jerry's number but it went to voicemail. "Hi Jerry, this is Holly Holcraft. Would you please give me a call when you have a chance? It's not about your house, just a personal issue. Thanks." I then let out a sigh and redialed the number. I just hate when people call and don't leave a clear and concise message. "Hi Jerry, this is Holly again. I'm sorry for bothering you but I was just wondering if you knew a guy named Amos Belroy? When you get this message would you give me a call back please? Thanks so much!"

Maybe I was tipping him off if he was the killer but I really couldn't believe he was and if he was, maybe he would call back just to find out what I knew, or stalk me and kill me. Okay, so maybe it wasn't a good idea but I couldn't take it back now.

Anger gripped me once again and just as tightly as I was gripping the steering wheel. I turned off halfway home and headed back into town, specifically to the hospital. No way was I going to let Betty get away with innuendos. I needed the truth. Was she the source that Travis had been talking to? He'd been right outside her hospital room door when I ran into him and he had looked surprised when I'd asked about Betty.

Pulling into the parking lot, I screeched into the first space I found and slammed my door closed. By the look on the receptionist's face, I must have looked pretty scary. Not wanting to alarm anyone and perhaps get myself thrown out, I took a moment to breathe and straighten my clothes. Giving my hair a quick toss, I put a smile on my face and slowly approached the reception desk.

"Hello, I would like to visit Betty Balmar, I believe she's in room 216, please."

The pretty brunette looked at her computer to confirm and then told me she needed to see if the doctor had finished and would be right back.

Hopefully, if the doctor was there it meant she would be able to leave soon. I crossed my fingers and hoped for the best. Not even ten minutes later, the receptionist came back with the doctor who approached me slowly, probably because he had to be over 80.

"Hello, Miss?" he asked as he reached for my hand.

"Holly, Holly Holcraft," I provided, extending my own hand. As we shook, he gently placed his other palm over our clasped hands.

"Miss Holcraft, I am so very sorry to tell you this, but Miss Balmar passed away this evening." I stared at him in disbelief, our hands frozen together until he lifted his away to reach into his pocket.

"Bu, but I just saw her," I managed to stutter. She couldn't be dead. She was so alive. It was then her words came back to me. "The doctors say that sometimes a person's body rallies at the end."

"Excuse me, Miss Holcraft?" I saw then that the doctor was extending an envelope to me. "Miss Balmar let me know that you would be coming by and asked me to give this to you when you did." He looked at the envelope sadly and then added, "Oh, and she said to make sure her sister doesn't find out."

I looked dumbly at the envelope he held until he finally reached out and placed it into my hand. All sorts of questions were running through my head but my lips wouldn't move to let them out so instead

I just nodded my head and left. What else could I do? Placing the envelope securely into my purse, I went to my car where I buried my head in my arms on the steering wheel and cried.

FRIENDS GIVE COMFORT

It was after midnight before I finally made it home. The moon was shining high in the sky, making spooky shadows through the tree branches. As I pulled into my driveway, my headlights swung around to illuminate Vana and Lucy sitting on my doorstep which nearly gave me a heart attack so I parked in the drive instead of the garage. A quick glance in my rear view mirror showed tear stains on my face which resisted my attempts to remove them. Giving up, I grabbed my purse, locked my car (bears you know) and walked up to my friends.

"What are you two doing here?"

"Well, you know, we just thought we'd get an early start on the morning," quipped Vana.

"Or a late end to the day," added Lucy. "What time is it?"

I gave a half laugh, "It's way too late and too early for either of those. Seriously, why are you sitting out here in the dark?"

The girls came over and gave me a hug. "Vana's friend at the hospital called us after you left."

"The receptionist," I said. "That's why she took so long to come back."

"Yeah, so we came over to wait for you, that way you couldn't tell us no," Vana confirmed. "Can we go inside? It's getting a bit cold out here and I think my butt is numb."

"You guys are just the best," I choked out with tears threatening again.

Vana grabbed our coats and dumped them on a chair while Lucy went into the kitchen. "Have you eaten?" she yelled back. "I'm just going to make us a snack," she said, answering her own question. Vana patted the couch cushion, "Come, sit. You look terrible."

Settling myself, I pondered what to say. I still hadn't opened the envelope from Betty yet. It's hard to read when your eyes are blurry with tears.

"Listen," began Vana, "I brought your box back. It's there in the corner." I looked over to where it sat by the door. I hadn't even seen her bring it in. "I didn't find anything, but I've got to say, that other woman that died looks familiar."

"What woman?"

"The other obituary, I don't know, she was some nondescript woman that died the same day."

Nondescript. That was the same word I had used. I remember thinking she had looked familiar too but the name wasn't. Was this an answer? I walked quickly over to the door and pulled the lid off the box. Grabbing the folder labeled 'obituaries' I found the one I wanted and let the rest of the papers slide out of the folder onto the floor. How could a woman who died ten years ago be familiar to Vana who I only met after moving here?

"Hey, what's going on?" Lucy asked as she came back into the living room. The face of the woman stared back at me and I studied the little details, a small mole above the right eyebrow and a tiny scar on the chin. "There were no pictures of the girls in the articles were there?" I asked as another thought struck me.

"Nope, which is kind of weird right?" questioned Vana.

"Pictures of what girls? What are you two talking about?" prompted a frustrated Lucy.

"I'm sorry, Lucy. Holly's husband died in a car accident 10 years ago," began Vana.

"I know that," Lucy interrupted, still holding the tray of snacks. Vana walked over and took it from her hands and set it on the coffee table. "The girls who caused the accident? There's no pictures of any of them in the papers."

"I didn't know that," she commented. "Something like that would take a lot of money to do."

"What would?" I said looking up from the picture.

"Keeping the girls' pictures out of the paper, someone had to pay them off and that takes money. A lot, because you're talking the paper, the cops, or someone who had the authority to do that," explained Lucy as she took the paper from me and looked at the picture. "That looks like Bonnie."

Vana and I both looked over Lucy's shoulder at the picture again. As I frowned at the grainy black and white photo, Vi was the first to speak. "I guess it could be, if you added years of anger lines to it. You know I read once that they do face transplants now. Do you suppose that's what happened? The paper said the driver went through the windshield, I would think that would just destroy your face."

I realized Lucy was waving her hand in front of my face. "Holly, are you there?"

I pressed my hands against my lips in shock and disbelief. When I spoke, my voice was just a whisper. "Are you telling me that Bonnie Balmar killed my husband?"

Vana and Lucy nodded at each other and then they each grabbed one of my arms and led me to the couch, Vana settling down next to me. "Let's set you down and talk about this. Lucy, would you get her a glass of wine please?"

"Why, why would she be mad at me? I should be angry with her. This doesn't make sense." My voice rose higher and higher with each word. Vana took the glass of wine from Lucy and pressed it into my hand.

"Take a nice long drink of this and, and we'll discuss it."

I took a sip and then sputtered, "This isn't wine."

"No, it's whiskey and you need it. Drink up," added Vana as she tipped the glass up, forcing me to drink it all.

Lucy sat on the other side of me and draped a blanket over our laps. "You've had quite the shock and we are staying the night with you. No arguments," she added as I opened my mouth to protest. "That's what friends do, they don't let friends stay alone."

A TRUTH REVEALED

At some point, they must have put me to bed because I woke hours later in the dark. The moon had set and only the night light in the bathroom illuminated my room. Ginger was snuggled up next to me taking nearly the entire bed. Apparently, she'd been stealing the snacks because the room definitely had an odor.

I snuck to the living room and retrieved my purse from the chair. The girls were snoring softly on the couches as I crept back to my room, shutting the door and grabbing a flashlight to read the letter by. The envelope bore my name on the outside and inside contained several sheets of paper.

> "My sister made me promise to take this to my grave, so I did. She chased away every boy I ever met, so I finally just gave up and instead put them into my novels. Ironically, she made me the secret success I am. She was so afraid of her secret coming out. But now I am gone and the truth can finally be revealed.

I was so shocked to run into you. I knew you lived here but my sister made me promise not to ever contact you, and I didn't, YOU knocked on MY door which I suppose was inevitable in a small town.

She has spent every moment of her life trying to destroy you but I don't know why. She moved here to follow you after the accident that killed your husband. After the face transplant, she was never the same. She used to be such a pretty girl and the donor wasn't. I told her she should be grateful she was still alive but it wasn't enough for her anymore.

My parents paid someone to destroy all the photos of her before the accident. They paid for therapists and psychologists but nothing helped. She became even worse after they died. I'm sure you want to know why I stayed with her despite her being so hateful. She blamed me for the accident, said it was my fault she was drinking and driving, said I should have stopped her and maybe I should have.

She was my sister, how could I leave her all alone? At the time I didn't know how hateful she was and then so much time had passed it was just too late. But she can't do anything to me now and you need to protect yourself. The things she has done. She's a hateful person. Please stay away from her.

Betty (Hope)

Poor Betty, having to live her life that way. At least she was free from her sister's clutches now

"What's her sister going to do now?" asked Vana. I shrieked, jumping out of my bed at the voice, not having realized that Vana had woken and was in my room. Ginger jumped up barking. "Great dog you are! How long have you been there?" I yelled at Vana with my hands clutched to my pounding heart. "Couldn't you at least let a person know before you sneak in?"

"Sorry, I thought you heard the door creak." She flicked the bedroom light on and my eyes watered at the sudden brightness.

"Did you read the whole thing?"

"Yeah," she said apologetically as Lucy rushed into the room holding a cast iron frying pan I use to make oven pancakes. We both looked at her puzzled.

"What?" she said. "I heard a scream and grabbed something heavy. My grandma always said cast iron pans would knock out a burglar."

"I'm sure they would," Vana remarked as she carefully removed the deadly weapon from Lucy's hand as I tried to calm the giant scared dog.

"So now you both know. I knew it wasn't Betty."

Lucy settled herself onto the bed next to me. "Did you think it might be?" she asked, concerned.

I shook my head and whispered, "never." It felt like there was a huge lump in my throat that the words were struggling to get past. "Travis said the driver had changed her name. He was trying to find someone who knew her. Betty. He was right outside her door when I took her flowers."

"Do you think he knew?" I shook my head again at her question. Vana sat on the other side of me and put her arm around my shoulders.

"This doesn't explain her animosity."

"Or her hiring Joe to undermine you." Lucy added.

Vana, ever the pragmatist, spoke the dreaded words. "So what do we do now?" I slipped out of their arms and stood up from the bed, turning to face the duo.

"She doesn't know we know. I think I need to confront her."

"Whoa, wait a minute," Lucy jumped in. "Is that the wise thing to do right now? Betty said she was dangerous."

I closed my eyes in frustration. What was the right thing to do? I'd never had an enemy before. And why did she hate me? "She killed my husband and injured her friends. Why is she mad at me?" Pacing back and forth with my hands clenched, I could feel the anger pulling at me again.

Neither one of my friends made a move to stop me. They must have realized they couldn't work this out for me. Some things you have to go through for yourself. Coming to a resolution, I was suddenly filled with exhaustion and collapsed on my bed letting my arms flop over my head. "I have to confront her. I need an answer from someone. Tomorrow. Right now we all need to go back to sleep. Being tired and cranky isn't going to help any of us."

Vana and Lucy headed for the door, "Okay, we'll be sleeping in the living room in case you need anything."

"Thanks, I know you will," I said as I sat up and smiled at them as I scratched Ginger's ears. "But I'll be fine. I've got my big scaredy dog to keep me safe."

Late the next morning I was awakened by a knock on my bedroom door followed by Vana's voice. "Hol, you awake? Escrow is calling." She held out my phone to me.

"Holly, this is Laura from escrow. There's a problem with the wire to Jerry Oates. We haven't been able to reach him. Can you see if you can get a hold of him?"

"Of course, I'm actually going to see Carol to get the rest of the keys. I'll ask her."

"Thanks Holly. I know he wants his money."

I hung up with Laura and called Jerry but the call just went through to voicemail so I called Carol.

"Carol, escrow can't reach Jerry, they said there was a problem with the transfer to his bank. Do you know where he might be?"

"Well, that's weird. Jerry said he was going to buy a car yesterday but I haven't heard from him since then."

"I just tried calling and it went straight through to voice mail which means it's probably off or dead. If you remember where he might have gone, please let me know and I'll keep an eye out for him. I'm sure he'll contact the escrow office once he realizes his money isn't there."

"Of course I will, that man is more trouble than he's worth," sighed Carol.

After hanging up with Carol I had a sudden thought.

"You know what I want to do?"

Both ladies looked at me and said, "what?" in unison.

"Let's go do that escape room."

"What? Now? I'm not even sure they're open on a weekday." Vana replied with a puzzled look on her face.

"Well call and find out because I need a break from all this craziness right now and an escape room sounds like a great idea."

Shrugging, Vana pulled out her phone and dialed the number which was actually answered.

"Hey, I was just wondering if you were open for business today? My friends and I would like to come by if you are." There was a long pause and then, "Great, we'll be there at 7. Thank you so much for accommodating us."

She disconnected the call and gave us the details. "She has a business group going through today but she said she would let us come in at 7 tonight. I told her four of us so we need to let Shelby know to come also."

"Awesome!" I exclaimed. "Finally something fun to look forward to."

Lucy gave me an odd look. "I thought you weren't into escape rooms," she said with a quick glance at Vana.

"Well today I am. Now get out of my house so I can get some work done and I'll meet you there, just text me the address. What?" I asked, looking at Vana's face.

"It's just that it's in Morecroft and I thought it would be more fun to go together?"

Shaking my head I responded, "fine. We'll go together." Vana was instantly happier. After they left, I tried to think of anything but Bonnie or Joe.

SAM'S ESCAPE ESCAPADES

Seven p.m. came sooner than expected and we pulled up at Sam's Escape Escapades, a quaint building that looked like the witch's house from Hansel and Gretel. It was probably a former house converted to a business. That seemed to happen a lot around here.

Shelby peered up at the building through the windshield. "This looks fun. Glad you asked me to come."

"Who else would we do this with?" asked Lucy as she got out of the driver's seat and shut the door behind her. "Quick, let's get a picture of all of us in front."

Joining her, we all got into our 'let's look slimmer and younger' pic poses and Lucy snapped a few shots.

Vana was practically jumping with joy. "Oooh this is going to be so much fun. You're going to love it."

"Yeah, I'm not too good at puzzles, sooo..." I said.

"Nah, they're easy. We'll figure it out together." Looping her arms through mine and Shelby's we walked through the front door. Lucy punched the lock button on the car and followed us inside.

Sam was a petite girl with short brown hair with golden highlights and deep brown eyes.

"Have we met before?" I asked her. "You seem familiar."

Sam laughed. "I don't think so. Welcome to Sam's Escape Escapades. "I've only got the Witches Tower open but it's the most popular. You've got 60 minutes to solve all the clues and unlock the door to escape." She handed us a walkie talkie. "If you get really stuck, you can use this to ask me for a clue but you ladies look pretty smart to me."

"Is the door really locked?"

"Of course not, that would be against fire codes but it's more fun if you think it is. There's a timer on the wall letting you know how much time you have left. So if you're ready, just step through this door and you can start."

"Oh, this is so exciting," Shelby said, rubbing her hands together as she stepped through the door.

Lucy and Vana followed her in and I brought up the rear. The room inside truly did look like the inside of a witch's tower with brick walls and a small stained glass window up near the top.

Vana immediately took charge. "Everyone spread out and yell if you see something that looks like a clue or a game." Stepping up to me she whispered, "this would have been much more fun on a date."

"Stop it," I whispered back.

The first clue we found was relatively simple, line up the correct phrases in the children's rhyme

Hickory Dickory Dock
The mouse ran up the clock
The clock struck 1, the mouse ran down
hickory dickory dock

We ran over to the clock over the fireplace and changed the hand to one o'clock and a small door popped open in the wall. The puzzles continued until we finally slid the last puzzle piece into place and out popped a key. Lucy grabbed it and shoved her fist into the air.

"Yes! We did it!" Walking over to the door, she slid the key in the lock and turned it and...nothing happened.

"Let me try," said Shelby. Lucy handed her the key and she jiggled it around a bit, turning the handle as she did so. She finally stepped back and hit the door with the palm of her hand. "Open up you stupid door!" she yelled at it.

Vana rolled her yes and grabbed the walkie talkie. We hadn't yet used it because we were stubborn and wanted to do things ourselves. "Hello? We're stuck in the room. Can you let us out?"

"Is it just me or does it seem like it's been longer than 60 minutes?" I asked the girls. We all looked at the digital clock but it still said there was five minutes left.

Shelby held up her wrist, "look it's really 9 o'clock. Where the heck is Sam?"

"I think I need to pee," said Lucy.

"Don't say that or we'll all have to go," I pleaded. Vana and Shelby banged on the walls and yelled for Sam but there was no response so Shelby laid down on the floor and peered under the crack in the door.

"The lights are all off out there," she whispered. "Do you think she forgot about us?"

"Oh great," signed Vana, "now we're stuck in a spooky witch's house."

"Uh, this was your idea," I pointed out.

"No, no, no, no. You wanted to come on a Tuesday night. I wanted to go on a busy Saturday."

Shelby put her hands on her hips and frowned. "I don't know. How do you forget you have customers?" Looking at Shelby something bothered me.

"Did she look familiar to you?" I asked.

Three pairs of eyes looked at me. "Well, now you mention it, she did look a bit familiar but I'm pretty sure I've never met her before," said Lucy. She went over to the sink and tried to look down the drain. "Do you think this is hooked up?"

"Why would there be a functioning sink in an escape room," I asked tiredly.

"I told you I need to pee. I could use the sink. It would serve her right for locking us up like this," she said angrily.

"Eww," we all said together. We all hurriedly pulled out our phones. "Ugh, no signal," I said.

"Me neither," added Lucy and Shelby together.

"Nope," said Vana, "but I'm going to try sending a text. Sometimes that works when the phone doesn't."

"Great idea." We all set about sending a text in the hopes someone would get a message. "Might as well make ourselves comfortable. We might be here for a while." I plopped myself down on the floor and leaned against the wall. "Too bad this wasn't the dwarfs house. I could use a couple of beds right now."

"Bet you're wishing you had a date right now," winked Vana conspiratorially from where she sat next to me. Lucy sat with her back to the sink and Shelby took the witch's chair.

"Actually I'm pretty glad I don't have to entertain a stranger right now. Especially if Lucy pees in that sink over there."

"Okay, I'll give you that. Where are you on the Oates investigation?"

"What are you talking about Jerry isn't dead." I answered.

"But Lionel is."

I sighed. "Travis doesn't know. There's no clues." I sighed.

"What?" They all asked together. I told them about my last meeting him.

"Oh."

We all lapsed into silence.

ESCAPING THE ESCAPE ROOM

"Didn't you say, these rooms all had two rooms to go through?" I questioned.

Liana pursed her lips, thinking. "I thought so but obviously there isn't," she said waving her hands around her.

"What if there is and she put us in the second room because the first room has an exit?"

"Okay, but why would the witch's house be the second room? Hansel and Gretel escape from the house."

"But they go into it from the woods," exclaimed Shelby scrambling to her feet. "I think you're right! Quick let's look around and find an exit from the other room."

The rest of us slowly rolled over onto our knees and used the wall to help us stand up as we were stiff from sitting for an hour.

Looking around Lucy said, "It can't be the wall with the window, obviously that's outside and the wall with the door doesn't make any sense either."

"That leaves the fake door or the oven," I added, glancing around.

"Hmm, the oven. Shelby turned the oven dial to 350 and pulled the extra large oven door open. "I think we need to climb through here," she said, looking at an opening in the back that wasn't there before.

"Why did you choose 350?" questioned Vana.

"I guess you don't cook much," responded Shelby.

"Not if I can help it."

"Most foods are cooked at 350. It had to be something," she added, shrugging her shoulders. "I'll go first."

She promptly bent over and crawled on all fours through the door. "It's the forest," she yelled back through the opening.

Vana threw up her hands. "Now that doesn't make any sense if that's the first room. It obviously has to be the second room."

"Great, it's the second room but if it is, then where was the clue to open the oven door?" I questioned.

Lucy bent down and yelled through the opening, "Is there a bathroom in there?"

"Are you ladies coming through or not?" Shelby yelled back. "And no, there's no bathroom, it's a freaking escape room. What do you expect?"

"It's okay Lucy," I said in all seriousness. "It's a forest, I'm sure there's a tree you can use."

She glared at me as she crawled through the oven. That left just me and Vana. "Age before beauty," I said, making a dramatic gesture to the oven door that would make a model proud.

"We're the same age nitwit," she said before climbing through. I followed her through and came out in a forest. Clearly the forest the kids escape to from the witch's house.

"Great, you're all here. Where's the key?" Shelby held her hand out for the key which none of us thought to bring. "Clearly, the key is supposed to open this door."

"Is it?" questioned Lucy. "I mean if this is the first room..."

"Which it's not," chimed in Vana turning to face the oven. "Look, it's a door. Wouldn't you escape through a door?"

"Exactly. Why escape through an oven?"

I jumped into the conversation, fearing otherwise we would be here all night. "Obviously they took creative license with the story. Just get the key and we'll see if it's the first door or the second door."

Lucy looked at the floor. "I think Shelby should go, she's younger and more agile than us."

Shelby pressed her lips together into a thin line. "I'm going but just because I want to get out of here." She walked over to the oven/door. "And don't think I won't hold this over your heads." A minute later she was back again with the key in hand. Walking over to the only remaining door, she inserted the key and turned. Turning back to us she made a grim face...and then pulled the door open.

"You brat!" I yelled at her as Lucy pushed us aside and made a mad dash down the hall looking for a restroom.

Shelby laughed. "Gotcha."

Lucy returned several minutes later and we all used the facilities. The place was deserted except for us. "Why would Sam do that?" I asked in the silence.

"I think I know." Lucy walked toward us with a picture in her hand. She held it up for us all to see.

"That's Joe and Sam," said Vana, taking the picture from Lucy. "She must be his sister."

"Oh great," I said. "Do you think she did this deliberately? Ugh."

"Well, you did fire him," pointed out Shelby, ever the observant one.

The front door had a push bar and we all left and jumped in Lucy's car.

"Is the door locked?" she asked.

Shelby made a face from the passenger seat. "Do you really care? It would serve her right if it wasn't."

"It's locked," I said as they all looked at me. "What? It's an automatic response when I leave to check if the door is locked."

"Realtor," Vana mocked me. We all jumped a moment later when Lucy screamed. Sam was illuminated in the headlights and she didn't look happy.

It was Sam from the escape room.

"You should go talk to her," said Vana, pushing me on the shoulder.

"By myself?"

She raised her eyebrows and shook her head, "I'm not going out there."

"Yeah, she looks scary," piped up Shelby.

"Hey bar girl. I thought you weren't afraid of anything," I retorted back.

"I said I wasn't afraid of the guys. But that chick. She's scary."

"Fine!" I got out of the vehicle and walked over to Sam.

"Sam. Maybe you can explain what the heck that was. Why would you deliberately lock us in?"

"You fired my brother. He's a really decent guy and you just FIRED him without getting his side. I came here because I want you to know what you did."

"Maybe you can explain and maybe I won't call the cops for locking us up in your business."

"He's confused."

"You can do better than that."

"No, really, he's confused. A former classmate from college ran into him and talked about how great their life was and how he should be embarrassed working for a woman. Didn't he have more dignity than that." She let out a long sigh and dropped her shoulders, defeated. "You know he transitioned right?"

"Yes. I do now. What does that have to do with it? Oh." It all seemed to make sense now.

"I see you understand. He was called weak his entire life but he saw how the men in the family were deferred to just because they were male. It only reinforced his desire to change. Then he ran into Bonnie and saw how assertive she was and how successful and, and behaving like a man she was and she convinced him you were just a weak female so he would despise you."

"He just 'happened' to run into a former classmate who just 'happened' to say the right thing to manipulate him into betraying me?"

Sam sighed and looked down at the ground and then finally, back up at me. "No. I think Bonnie found out about him and deliberately brainwashed him. I know she met him last summer at a party. I think she's been working on him this whole time. I'm really sorry for what I did but you need to understand that I'm very protective of him. And I didn't realize how evil Bonnie is."

I looked at Sam, considering. "I'll understand why you did what you did. It doesn't make it okay. But I understand. Thank you for coming to talk to me."

By the time we got home it was well after midnight and it took all my effort to get undressed and tucked into bed. Despite the late hour, Ginger had still insisted on a quick trip outside and a treat before bed. Now snuggled next to her warm body, questions kept pestering me. Irritation at the situation helped me make up my mind about one thing though, I definitely was going to pay a visit to Bonnie tomorrow. Another thought occurred to me and, although it was late, I felt it couldn't wait.

CONFRONTATION

Walking into Bonnie's office the next day, I slammed the obituaries on her desk. It had taken me all morning to work up my courage to come see her. "Why did you do it Bonnie?"

She looked at the picture in the paper and then spat at me. "So you finally figured it out. Took you long enough."

"I don't understand what you blame me for," I snapped back.

Bonnie wrinkled her nose as if she smelled something bad. "At a check up, the nurse said, 'it was a shame you didn't get the other woman but she understood why the husband wouldn't want it to happen.' The doctors kept telling me it was a one shot chance. It didn't make any sense to me. Until the bandages came off. You took everything from me," she cried angrily.

"What are you talking about?" I yelled dumbfounded.

"My face!" she snarled. "You and your big mouth. I was supposed to get Laura Wexler's face and you told her husband not to do it."

"What are you talking about?" I asked, repeating myself.

"Instead I'm ugly! Because of you!" Bonnie continued on as if I hadn't even spoken. Her face was red with rage and spit flew from her lips as she spoke. What had I done?

"Why would I do that? I've never met Laura Wexler."

Bonnie's face suddenly smirked with understanding. "You don't know do you?"

"I know that you've been undermining my business since you moved here. I understand that you hired my assistant to sabotage me. What I don't know is, why?" Bonnie's face was so red it was actually turning purple. Small white scars showed through the redness around the edge of her face.

"Oh, my God, Bonnie. Did you hide bones at Carol's place to frame her just to sabotage my transaction?" I cried horrified at the lengths she would go.

"What if I did? You can't do anything about it. And, you have no proof. You've already besmirched my good name by accusing me of hijacking your listing appointment with the Hotchkisses. No one will even listen to you now."

"I never actually went to the board. I only mentioned it to Joe, who clearly passed it on to you." I gave half a laugh. "You sabotaged yourself on that one. And what do you mean I haven't suffered? You killed my husband because of your poor decisions."

"One moment doesn't compare to a lifetime of humiliation," she snarled. "Do you think it was luck we live in the same town? I followed you here! You're always putting your two cents in where it's not wanted."

"Stop trying to mess with me Bonnie and stay out of my life you selfish, self-centered...." my voice ran out and I walked out before she could answer and slammed the door behind me. I left my car behind and just kept walking oblivious to everything around me. My heart was racing and my hands were clenched into tight fists. "Aarrgh," I screamed.

What could I do? Bonnie killed my beloved husband and there was nothing I could do about it. Lydia's words kept echoing through my head. "She hasn't broken any laws." What had she actually done besides using delaying tactics on my transactions and hiring my assistant away from me? All the guilt would lie with Joe. Bonnie would deny it all. Tears began to drip down my cheeks. My vision blurred and I suddenly stopped as I collided with a parked car, except I could see it wasn't actually parked.

"Holly, are you alright?" It was Travis's vehicle. "I've been trying to get your attention. What's wrong? Look, I'm sorry about the other day. I didn't mean what I said." He wrapped his arms around me as I broke down into his arms. Sobs punctuated my words as I told him the whole story. Finally, running out of tears, I took a step back as I was met with silence and looked at him. "Travis?"

Held me at arms length. "Look Holly, I wanted to tell you. I've tried to tell you several times."

"Tell me what?"

He took a deep breath and let it out slowly before speaking. "Laura Wexler was my wife. I'm the husband who spoke to you about the face transfer. I'm the reason Bonnie is angry at you."

I stepped back out of his arms and stared at him. What was he saying? His words didn't make any sense to me.

"You knew all this time and you didn't say anything?"

"I tried, I didn't realize at first, not until you asked me to investigate and then I realized it was the same accident. My wife was in the front passenger seat where the impact was. She died instantly. "

"Laura Wexler?"

"Yes, she kept her maiden name for work."

How could he be that guy? I would have remembered him. Why were so many people lying to me? What did I do wrong that so many people hated me?

"I need to think," I said as I turned and began walking away. Travis put his hand on my shoulder to stop me. "At least let me drive you somewhere," he began but I shook him off.

"No! Just leave me alone."

I heard him say, "Holly," as I walked away and then his car started and drove away leaving me alone again. Alone with my thoughts and suddenly I didn't want to be alone and I certainly wasn't going back to Bonnie's to get my car. Fishing my phone out of my pocket, I made a call.

Vana arrived a few minutes later to pick me up and after wiping the tears from my eyes, I updated her on with the new information as we sat in her car.

"How did you not know it was him in the chapel?"

"I was distraught. I didn't care who it was and it was ten years ago."

"Wait, you said his wife was an organ donor?"

"Yeah, I'll never forget that. He said his wife was a donor and the driver of the car needed a face transplant. I remember I said I couldn't imagine knowing that my wife's killer was walking around with her face. I didn't even remember that until Travis reminded me of it."

Vana pursed her lips.

"What?" I cried.

"I think you've made an enemy for life."

"Bonnie? I guess I always had one, I just didn't know it." I twisted my hands in my lap as I stared out the windshield.

"I'm going to take him back."

"Travis?"

"Joe."

Vana couldn't contain her shock. "You're taking him back?"

Sighing, I took a deep breath. This was likely to take a long time to make her understand and, quite frankly, I didn't understand myself. Maybe it was because of all the drama lately, I didn't know why actually but it just felt right.

"Everybody deserves a second chance. He was misguided but he's still young."

"How are you going to trust him?"

"I gave him a call. We had a long talk and came to an understanding. Plus motivation is a huge thing and he was pretty shocked by how evil a person can be and I don't think he wants to become that person."

"Well, if you're sure, but keep an eye on him. Although."

"Although what?"

"You don't have a good track record with assistants and he's been good for an exceptionally long time. Well, until the last couple weeks," she clarified.

"He's only been here for six months," I exclaimed.

"Yes, that's exactly my point. None of the others lasted longer than two," she pointed out.

I tried hard not to whine, but failed miserably. "Although what?"

"You don't have a good track record with assistants and he's been good for an exceptionally long time. Well, up until the last couple weeks," she clarified.

"He's only been here for six months," I exclaimed.

"Yes, that's exactly my point. None of the others lasted longer than two," she pointed out.

"I'm breaking the assistant curse. Besides, he understands he's on probation and he can only work in the office when I'm there. He really was a good assistant before he strayed."

She patted my knee. "Good. Now let's go get a drink."

I snuggled down into my bed, my beast of a dog laying across the foot, but I couldn't get to sleep. Something had been bothering me all day, 'tickling my brain,' as my mom used to say. I wondered if Carol had managed to reach Jerry. At the end of the day, we all want our money. I hope he got his car. Was he buying Mike's car? It was the same as the one he drove in the movies. Maybe that was why he washed it. I sat bolt upright in bed.

Mike washed his car again. The car that doesn't run. Why? What was that Amos said? A car will run without a battery in it as long as you keep it running.

Jerry!

I called Travis while I was dressing, hoping I wouldn't be too late.

THE THINGS NIGHTMARES ARE MADE OF

A light rain was falling as I backed my car down the driveway. Carol and Betty's houses were both dark, Carol because she had moved and Betty, well I didn't want to think about that right now. I drove past Mike's house and around to the road in the back. I'd noted that the bushes in the back blocked the view of the road from the houses and I cut my lights as I pulled in and parked. The only illumination came from the street lights as I crept my way through his back property, my rain boots getting sucked into the mud. No wonder Carol's truck got stuck in this stuff.

Rounding the corner of his house, I tried the handle to his garage and thankfully, it was unlocked. Using the light on my phone, I shone it around the car. Up under the edge of the wheel well, I found what I was looking for.

"What are you doing in here?"

I jumped startled at the voice. Mike was standing in the darkened doorway from the house. He flicked on the light, blinding me.

"Where's Jerry?" I demanded.

Mike got a smirk on his face and gave a half hearted laugh. "What makes you think I know where that fat jerk is?"

"Why do you hate him so much?" I asked instead. A noise behind me caught my attention but then there was nothing but the sound of the rain falling.

Mike took a step into the garage. "Are you always this snoopy?"

"Well that depends. If you ask my daughter, yes. If you ask my friends, no." Glancing around, there were tools on a bench but it was too far away to be helpful so I kept the open door at my back.

"Jerry said he told me he was buying a car. His wife has a picture of him from the movies standing behind one that looks exactly like yours. It had to be your car and now no one has heard from him."

"He's probably camping again with his money from the house. Carol told me it closed escrow," he jeered.

"Except he's not. You're not very good in the luck department are you? You didn't know he went camping when you killed Lionel and you don't know that there was a problem with the wire. He hasn't received the money from the house yet."

A panicked look passed over his face briefly. "I didn't kill Lionel. I don't even know him."

"Maybe not. You planned on killing Jerry Saturday night but you didn't know he went camping. You also didn't know that the pipes in Carol's yard weren't buried deep enough. Betty told her, that's why she buried her dead animals there. It started raining Saturday night and that's why you cut the drone lesson short. When you cut across the back of Carol's yard, the truck broke the pipe. The leaking water washed the bones into Betty's yard and the truck got stuck.You must've been pretty panicked when the cops showed up."

"You don't know what you're talking about lady. How could I have killed Lionel if the truck was stuck?"

"Because you took the battery out and started your car with it early Sunday morning then took the back road to get out of town so no one would see you. Is that why you killed Amos? Because he would have figured it out? I know you and he were in the same support group, him for a football injury, you for the stunt work. How many people have you killed Mike? I mean besides, Lionel, Amos and Jerry."

"Jerry's not dead."

"You know he is. Escrow called and asked me to check on him. I suspect he's in Carol's back yard, buried with her animals."

"You're crazy, you know that? You got no proof for any of this."

"The hose was leaking, you washed off the car after driving through the mud so no one would see you and you had to clean off your 'non working' car. The mud would be a dead giveaway. That and the lights could have only shone into Betty's window when you were coming back down the hill. There's a slight gap in the brush behind her house that would only allow light through from that one direction. Guess you should have turned your lights off, but then again it being a classic car and all."

Mike ran his fingers along the edge of the car as he slowly stepped around the vehicle, holding a tire iron in his hand. The rain was pounding down harder now, nearly as hard as my heart was pounding. He gave a small laugh. "You're crazy lady, you know that? First you accuse me of doing something to Jerry and now you think I killed Lionel and Amos..."

Whatever he was going to say next was drowned out by a high pitched scream from an angry woman. Gloria was in the door with a big branch held over her head. "You killed my Lionel!" she screamed as she lunged for him. Unfortunately she missed but the board hit the car and left a huge dent in it.

"What are you doing! That's a classic! You're gonna pay for that!" Mike screamed. Not paying attention to Mike's hysterics, Gloria leaped over the hood like in one of those action movies and swung the board at Mike's head. Panicked, he looked at me and then dove under her arm and hit the garage door opener. As it slowly crept up he rolled under the edge.

This only infuriated Gloria more and she slammed the branch against the door until it was high enough to get through. "I'll kill you, you, you jerk!" she screamed after him.

I dialed 911 on my phone and ran after them, at which point the power went out causing me to misjudge the distance, and I slammed my head into the bottom of the half open door. Rubbing my head, I carefully ducked underneath.Outside the moon peeked out from behind a cloud illuminating Mike scrambling away from Gloria on all fours. He made it to the porch but his front door was locked and he was trapped. As she circled around him, he dodged to his right landing in a huge puddle by his front walkway.

"Admit it. You killed my Lionel!" she screamed at him and waved the board threateningly but careful to maintain her distance away from him.

Mike threw his hands up. "Okay, fine. I killed him. It was supposed to be Jerry, he can't even die right! I was his stunt man for his television series. His stupid bailout from the car gave me permanent brain concussion. We all asked him to change it, but nooo, not Jerry. It was his signature move." He said mockingly, pausing to take a breath, when he continued it was in a lower voice.

"I lost everything, my wife, my kids. All because of him and his stupid stunt causing brain trauma. He made me who I am today. A nobody," he snarled.

"Why did you kill Amos?"

"You were right. Amos was in my brain trauma support group. About a month ago I told him how my classic car was stuck outside because I couldn't afford a freaking battery. He told me you could actually drive a car once it was started without the battery in it and he would come over and give me a jump so I could get it in the garage. It got me thinking but I couldn't let him ruin it for me. I saw his truck on the side of the road and I put a small hole in the brake line. It's Jerry's fault Amos died, because I couldn't even afford to buy a freaking battery!"

Standing in the road, I had a view up and down the street and way down the road I could see a street light flickering on.

"And then you hoped Carol would take the fall. The finger bone was a nice touch. Where did you get it?"

"She's an idiot, certainly too stupid to figure it out," Mike said laughing. "That pig in her garage wasn't the first one. Who knows what they eat. How did you figure it out?"

The light down from Betty's house started flickering.

"Amos told me the same thing about the battery, probably because it was fresh in his mind from helping you. Carol would never drive over her pets graves, but you didn't know that. That's how I knew it was you. That and the fact that no one would wash a garaged car twice in one week."

"You bastard, yelled Gloria. "I loved him and you took him from me!" Gloria lunged again at Mike who ducked to avoid it. Putting his hand back for balance, the metal bar almost came in contact with the exposed wires as the streetlight in front of the house flickered into life but a blur knocked him out of the way.

"I told him he needed to fix that. Why would he leave the power on to the light?"

Gloria looked at me and smiled as the board dropped from her fingers. "I guess when the power went out he tried to flip switches and turned the wrong one on."

My eyes went wide, "Did you...? Never mind, I don't want to know." In the distance we could hear the faint sound of a police siren.

Shocked, I shined my phone light on him.

Travis was lying on top of Mike and they both looked to be unconscious.

"Gloria, go shut off the power!" I yelled alarmed. It seemed like forever before she came back and reported it was off. I dashed over and pulled Travis off Mike as the first police car pulled up. He had an erratic pulse but was breathing. Without an external defibrillator there was nothing I could do for him but there was something I could do for Jerry.

Rain was pelting my face in the pitch black and my shoes sank into the ground with every step I took. Thankfully it hadn't started until after the electricity was turned off. My jacket was soaked through by the freezing rain and my hand holding the phone shook so badly I was afraid of losing it. Between the power outage and the rain, my vision was severely limited, the light from my phone reflecting off the rain instead of illuminating the ground but I figured I had to be close to the right spot. It was confirmed with my next step, when my foot sank down in the mud up to my knee. I fell on my hands and knees into the mud, dropping my phone, which landed upright illuminating a tiny skull. It looked like a cat skull.

Feeling around some more I felt a hand. Shoving the edge of the phone in my mouth, I bit down to hold it steady and felt my way up the arm to a shoulder and then Jerry's head. I breathed a huge sigh of relief that his head was above the ground. He must have been able to dig himself out or Mike did a terrible job, which wouldn't be surprising.

A groan came from Jerry as I tried to pull him up. "Shhh, it's me Holly. I'm here to help you. Can someone help me!" I screamed. "Help! I need medical assistance!" I kept yelling hoping that someone would hear me from Carol's backyard.

"Hey! Who's out there?" came back to me.

"It's me Holly. I've got Jerry Oates here. He's hurt. I need paramedics."

"We're coming." Shortly after, the light from several flashlights began bouncing off the trees and bushes. A paramedic and several officers arrived and worked to pull Jerry from the mud. Their flashlights illuminated the area showing just how fortunate Jerry was to have managed to survive. The mud pit was huge and Jerry was still buried from the waist down. There was no way I would have gotten him out.

"How's Travis?" I asked the first officer to arrive. "Dave said he's going to be okay." He gave a nod to the paramedic. "The ambulance should be here shortly. If you hurry, you can go with him."

"Thanks," I replied, getting to my feet and hurrying back to Mike's house.

Travis was still unconscious as I knelt by his side and held his hand. "He's going to be okay," said a man in plain clothes holding an umbrella. "They used an IED to get his heart back to normal. Dave said he'll be fine. We're just waiting on the ambulance."

"Thanks so much. I'm Holly. The others are helping Jerry. Mike tried to kill him and he's killed several other people as well. Wha...what happened to him? Is he...?"

"He's still alive. Too bad for him. He'll be in jail for a long time."

I nodded still watching for any signs from Travis but his eyes were closed. At least he was still breathing and alive. My emotions were all over the place. I wanted him to live with all my heart but part of me was still angry with him. My thoughts were interrupted by the detective.

"I'm detective Martin, by the way. You probably didn't notice me but I was behind you in line at the store when that lady was giving you grief over the donuts. Great job with her by the way."

I felt my face flush. I was embarrassed and proud at the same time.

"I hope you don't mind if I say so, but you give blondes a bad name."

"Oh, why is that?" I asked, ready to be offended.

"You're smart. I think you're secretly super smart like Marilyn Monroe. I can see what Travis see's in you."

"Oh, well thanks I guess. Wait, he talks about me?" Sirens filled the air as the ambulances got closer.

"Mmhmm. I think you should talk to him about that." The sirens of the arriving ambulances drowned out any other conversation but only gave way to more thoughts and confusion about

Travis.

As the paramedics loaded Travis into the ambulance, the other paramedic and officers brought Jerry around the house on the stretcher. He was coated in mud and the only clean areas were where they had IV lines inserted in his arm.

"How is he?" I asked.

"He's extremely lucky. If he wasn't such a big guy, he probably wouldn't have been able to get out of the mud. That, and the fact that you found him in time." said the paramedic. He nodded in the direction of the ambulance that was driving away as a second one pulled in. "They get Travis off okay?"

"Yes," I said, relieved. "That's him leaving now and I'm glad Jerry is ready to go too. It's getting pretty cold out here."

As the stretcher passed by, Jerry made them stop. "Thank you Holly. I'm going to tell everyone that you're the best agent ever. You really go above and beyond for your clients."

"Well, thank you Jerry but you'd better get off to the hospital yourself. Oh, and Jerry," I called after him, "escrow has an issue with your bank account. I'll check on you tomorrow so we can get that fixed." They loaded him in the ambulance and one of the attendants wrapped a warm blanket around me.

"You can ride with us," he said. "You probably need to get checked out yourself." Now that I had the blanket around me, I began shivering. He was probably right, so I just nodded and climbed in the back, settling on the bench. Warm air never felt so good. My timing couldn't have been more perfect as through the window, I was rewarded by the sight of officer Moran pulling up to the house.

A HAPPY ENDING

Three days later, the girls and I met for lunch at Katie May's. I really just needed some hometown comfort with my girls and good food after the disastrous week I'd had.

"So Jerry's okay?" Inquired Shelby.

"Yes. We got to him in time and Mike's in jail, where he'll stay for the rest of his life."

"And Travis?" she said said in a come hither voice.

"He's fine but I'm not currently talking to him."

"Why not?" she demanded.

"I just can't. It's too much, the whole Bonnie thing. He's just a reminder of my husband's death. Oh, and Bonnie is getting reprimanded." I smiled at that thought.

"For what?" asked Lucy.

"The Hajari's filed a complaint because Bonnie didn't advise them of the appointment. Apparently, they had informed her of his morning workouts. She said she forgot. All her files are going to be monitored for the next few months."

"And Carol?"

"Oh, oh, I know that one," cut in Lucy. "She headed off to her fellowship in Africa."

"She's what?"

"My friend at the recorder's office told me she's got a fellowship to study ancient artifacts in Africa."

"Is she really qualified for that?" asked Shelby. "You said she was pretty cuckoo." She emphasized the word by swirling her finger around her ear.

She was cuckoo. Super smart something piqued my memory. "The detective said I gave blondes a bad name because I was super smart."

The ladies looked at me confused. "Okay," said Vana. "That's weird but nice?"

"The detective, the night we rescued Jerry. That's what he said. What if Carol is secretly smart?"

Lucy picked up her sandwich to take a bite as she said, "Well she does have a degree in archeology."

Wine shot through my nose at the information. "The finger bone," exclaimed Vana and I in unison. "What if the farm is just an excuse to smuggle artifacts?" she asked excitedly.

"Oh, no no no no no," I said. "I don't care what she did. That transaction is done and I never want to revisit it again."

A chicken salad and two glasses of wine later, I said my goodbyes and stepped out into the late autumn afternoon. Although the breeze was cool, the sunshine on my face felt wonderful as I closed my eyes to enjoy the feeling.

"Excuse me miss." I opened my eyes to a rather staid gentleman walking a dog. "Would you be Miss Holly Holcraft?"

"Yes, I would be. And you are?"

"I would rather not say, but if you hurry, you might be able to catch Mr. and Mrs. Hotchkiss as they walk their dogs along the docks. It's my understanding, they are in desperate need of a real estate agent as their last one has been fired."

Stunned, I just stupidly said, "They what?" He must think I'm a total idiot. Instead he handed me the dog leash and said, "let's just agree that we never met. Now hurry along, So kind of you to take your neighbor's dog for a walk." And then he winked at me.

A hand smacked me on the back and I jumped. "You're not going to just stand there and blow another chance are you?" Asked Vana.

"You really need to stop doing that," I said with my free hand on my chest. "You're gonna kill me. Okay dog, let's go." I hurried across the street and over to the docks, scanning the area for the Hotchkisses when I realized I didn't actually know what they looked like. Smacking my forehead, I pulled out my phone and did a quick online search but I needn't have bothered.

"Hello. Are you Holly Holcraft?" I was asked for the second time in ten minutes. An older lady and her husband were walking a pair of small shaggy dogs. She reached out her hand to me. "It is you. I recognize you from your picture on the packet you sent to us."

I smiled and shook her hand. "I'm so glad you received it," Mrs. Hotchkiss."

"Call me Alma. Is this your dog?" she asked bending down to pet it. "What's his name?"

Oh shoot I didn't! "Oh no, this is my neighbor's dog. I'm just doing him a favor."

"Oh it's Bernard," she said, fumbling with the tag on his collar as I breathed a silent sigh of relief. "He is quite adorable. Most people think we should have pedigree dogs, but I prefer mutts myself. So much better behaved and healthier overall."

Standing up, she looked me in the eye and continued on. "I believe everyone deserves second chances. Your assistant called and explained everything. If you are willing to give him a chance, then I certainly think I should do the same. Well that and the dog tried to bite Bonnie. I guess they judge character better than we do." she laughed. "You know what, we already have a buyer, you can handle the paperwork. I was going to have the attorney do it, but you've got spunk. And I'm going to recommend you to all my friends."

"Thank you," I managed to stammer out flabbergasted. I could just imagine real steam coming out of Bonnie's ears. "I will do my absolute best for you. And your dogs are adorable."

"Thank you. I'll messenger all the paperwork over to you and we can do electronic signatures. You will be at the inspections in person?" she asked, arching her eyebrow. I felt my face flush.

"Yes, of course I will. I am usually very good at this." Alma laughed again, a light tinkly laugh that made me feel like everything was right in the world. She touched her husband's arm as I looked at him.

"Oh don't worry about Albert. He agrees with everything I want."

"What she said," he added.

WHAT'S NEXT FOR HOLLY?

Holly has been nominated to serve as chairman of the annual Fall Festival. It's a great honor until she finds out that the previous chairman is dead and his body found in the lake. Yes, the lake which also happens to be the site of the festival.

The event is now moved to the site of the Blume house, which is totally not haunted. Still mourning over the loss of a friend, will she be able to pull off the festival and still keep her business going?

Sign up for my newsletter at MRDollschniederAuthor.com and be the first to be notified when Fear at the Fall Festival is published. You'll also receive a free story, Mildred, the elderly owner of the town's candy shop.

ABOUT THE AUTHOR

M.R. Dollschnieder has over a decade in real estate and nearly 20 years writing for local newspapers. She lives in the California desert with her husband, two dogs, three cats and six chickens.

She spends her days in front of the computer writing and fending off the cats' attempts to assist her by sitting on the keyboard and standing in front of the monitors.

Don't miss out!

Visit the website below and you can sign up to receive emails whenever M R Dollschnieder publishes a new book. There's no charge and no obligation.

https://books2read.com/r/B-A-QLKLB-NMHID

BOOKS 2 READ

Connecting independent readers to independent writers.

www.ingramcontent.com/pod-product-compliance
Lightning Source LLC
LaVergne TN
LVHW091046080826
845145LV00002B/641

* 9 7 8 1 9 6 4 4 6 3 0 0 1 *